THERE were so many things Susan had to think about. She had already announced that she meant to have nothing to do with her granduncle's scheme to set her and her twin in competition for a fortune—and Oliver's love.

Nonetheless, Susan knew she could not stop herself from falling in love with Oliver. Yes, she *would* call him Oliver in her thoughts! Even though she was certain she would never be able to say his name to his face. . . .

Also by Georgina Grey:

| | | |
|---|---|---|
| FRANKLIN'S FOLLY | 50026 | $1.75 |
| THE HESITANT HEIR | 23582 | $1.50 |
| TURN OF THE CARDS | 23969 | $1.75 |

Buy them at your local bookstore or use this handy coupon for ordering.

This offer expires 2/4/81                    8999

# BOTH SIDES
## of the
# COIN

Georgina Grey

FAWCETT COVENTRY • NEW YORK

BOTH SIDES OF THE COIN

Published by Fawcett Coventry Books, a unit of CBS Publications, the Consumer Publishing Division of CBS, Inc.

ISBN: 0-449-50043-8

Selection of the Doubleday Romance Library, February, 1980

Printed in the United States of America

First Fawcett Coventry printing: May 1980

10  9  8  7  6  5  4  3  2  1

For
Eleanore

# Chapter 1

"How frightfully quaint London seems to me now," Lady Hammerhead announced, peering suspiciously into her china cup with the air of someone whom nothing could surprise. "So terribly insular after Paris."

"Is the tea made to your satisfaction, my dear Lucinda?" Lady Tangle inquired weakly, half hoping to be told that something was swimming in it, if that would mean she should avoid another endless recitation of the splendors of Paris under the newly established reign of the Emperor Napoleon.

"Since you have been drinking it, my dear Dorothy," Lady Hammerhead said tartly, "you know as well as I do that it is dreadful as usual. I assure you that the sort of service we have endured these past two weeks would not be countenanced for a single hour on the Rue St. Germaine."

As she made this pronouncement, Lady Hammerhead sat up very straight indeed, as though to give evidence to the fact that she had spent two hours a day as a girl strapped to a backboard which was only one of the many details of her exemplary girlhood which she constantly offered as proof that standards were slipping and would, no doubt, continue to slip until the English had reached that general level of slovenliness that they seemed to enjoy so much. A thin, angular woman with a nose like the side of a knife, she was dressed in the latest French fashion in a gown of green velour with a high lace collar which accentuated the length of her stemlike neck.

Lady Tangle was as unlike her as possible, being a plump, slightly dowdy personage with very red cheeks and a plaintive expression.

"I believe that cook does the best she can to oblige," she said now, "although, I must say that you have quite put her out of temper with all your talk of French cuisine. After all, there is a limit to what one can expect from servants hired on a temporary basis."

Lady Hammerhead placed her cup and saucer on the mahogany tea table which stood between them and began to assault the air with her ivory paneled fan.

"You might have brought your own people down from the country," she declared impatiently.

"Simply because it was necessary for us to rent a house in London for the season does not mean that we must live like barbarians."

Lady Tangle began to fiddle nervously with nothing in particular, despite the fact that her friend had had frequent occasion to tell her that the habit drove her to distraction and beyond. It had been a great strain on her to have been cast into such an intimate relationship with this overbearing lady whose relationship to her was so tenuous on the one hand and so firm on the other, their nieces being the only real bond between them.

"I believe that I have explained," she said with the resignation of one who has not really been listened to before and would, no doubt, succeed to be heard no better in the future, "that Susan and I live quite simply in Somerset. Why, the few servants we have would have been as much out of place here in London as—as daffodils in a bowl of orchids."

"What a turn you have for queer similes, my dear Dorothy," Lady Hammerhead said with a thin smile. "I can quite understand why Lord Tandem was looking at you in such a peculiar manner when you sat beside him at supper the other evening at Almack's."

"Oh, dear!" Lady Tangle exclaimed with such a hopeless note in her voice that the black and white bulldog who had been slumbering peacefully beside her wing chair raised his bullet-shaped head and began to growl.

In response, the silver gray poodle which had been languishing at Lady Hammerhead's side began to yelp convulsively.

"Now see what you have done!" his mistress declared. "You know what Lulu's nerves are!"

"Be quiet, Reginald, do!" Lady Tangle pleaded as the bulldog began to heave himself to his feet in a determined fashion. It was not the first time in the past two weeks that he had given evidence of a strong desire to put Lulu's nerves to rest forever, and although Lady Tangle would never have admitted it aloud, she felt a certain sympathy with him.

"Ah, well," Lady Hammerhead said when the two animals were quiet once again, "I expect that we must learn to be patient with one another. After all, we share a great responsibility."

With that, at least, Lady Tangle could agree heartily. Six years ago when her sister and her husband had been tragically killed in a coaching accident, she had anxiously taken on the care of one of their two children, a delightful little girl named Susan. And, although she had never had children herself and had been already, at that time, widowed, the experiment had worked even better than she had dared to dream. Susan and she had suited one another from the first, and the girl had seemed quite content to settle down in the country with her horses and her dogs, even though she had at first, quite naturally, expressed some distress at having been separated from her twin sister.

It had been Lady Hammerhead who had insisted that the girls be parted, and as was usual, she had had any number of good reasons. In the first place, it was clearly not fair that her brother's children both be given up to the maternal side of the family. If, in fact, dear departed Albert had made his wishes clear in writing before his death, she was certain that he would have wanted both girls to be provided with her civilizing influence. There was also the argument that Penelope, even at the age of eleven, showed no propensity for a bucolic existence and was far more interested in joining her paternal aunt in the continental forays which Lady Hammerhead had proceeded to indulge in as soon as the nuisance of the French Revolution had been tidied away.

So it had been that for the past six years the twin sisters had been brought up in considerably different worlds. While Susan had educated herself at leisure in the vast library at Tangle Hall, without the aid of so much as a governess, Penelope had willingly endured the rigors of a "lady's" education, which meant that she had become proficient in French and Italian and could play the pianoforte with a certain artificial flare. That she had learned anything else except for a certain worldly wise manner and an overwhelming interest in fine clothing and the doings of the *haut ton* abroad was not at all clear to Lady Tangle, although Lady Hammerhead had assured her often enough during the past weeks that it was a pity that poor Susan must

11

be put in such direct contrast as Penelope's "polish" provided.

But although the girls differed considerably in their interests and achievements, there was one regard in which no comparison between them could be drawn. When Lady Hammerhead and her charge had arrived at the rented house in Grosvenor Square fresh from their Parisian whirl, the butler, Duggin, had announced them with the breathless air of one who had seen a ghost. And, although Lady Tangle should have expected a resemblance, even she had been taken aback when she had seen the mirror image of her Susan enter the drawing room, bedecked in the latest French fashion. Indeed, had it not been for the fact that Susan was wearing the simplest of muslin frocks, she could not have known which was which.

The girls themselves had taken their extraordinary similarity in good part, although, after their first tentative embrace, Lady Tangle had noticed them looking at one another in a curious sideways fashion that ladies often employed when looking at themselves in a mirror in public.

As soon as she and Susan were alone again their guests having been taken to their rooms, the girl had hurried to recount her sensations.

"Of course I knew from the miniature that Mama left that Penelope and I looked very much alike," she said. "But I do not think we did as much then as now. Why, we seem to have grown toward one another, although, no doubt, that is a very awkward way of putting it."

There had been a certain defiance even then in her voice, brought on, no doubt, by her Aunt Lucinda's comments, which had charmingly made clear the fact that she was shocked to see her other niece so frightfully *déclassé*.

"But we will put all that right," she had assured Lady Tangle as she and Penelope had prepared to leave the room. "No doubt you did your best, my dear Dorothy. Our French maid, Annette, will do wonders with the poor girl's hair, as you shall see, and I have been given the name of an excellent dressmaker. Of course it will be quite impossible to put a polish on her manners with the season about to start, but one will do one's best, and I am certain that Penelope will be able to offer all manner of advice.

No wonder Susan's pride had been wounded, Lady Tangle thought.

"You are not in the least awkward," she had told Susan. "Oh, dear! Oh, dear! If I had expected anything like this, I would never have agreed that you and your sister should have a joint coming-out."

"Never mind, Aunt Dorothy," Susan had consoled her. "We have only to hold the line. No one will lay a hand on my hair without my consent, and as for dressmakers, I am already perfectly well outfitted."

And yet, although Susan had spoken with her usual strength of purpose, Lady Tangle had seen

13

the worried lines between her eyes as she had peered at herself in the glass above the mantelpiece and known that she was seeing Penelope looking back at her.

Indeed, the first time the sisters had appeared in public together, they had made a sensation.

"Twin jewels, eh?" Sir Harold Seecome had declared to Lady Tangle, with a connoisseur's satisfaction in his rheumy old eyes, to one of which he had applied his quizzing glass. "Not a shade of difference in the hair, eh? Spun gold for both of 'em. Eyes matching brown. Extraordinary, eh? Same tilt to the nose. Charming! Charming! Alike as two peas in a pod!"

Lady Tangle silently rejoiced that she could see a difference. She had hoped that clothing alone would make it quite clear which sister was which, but in that she had, surprisingly enough, been disappointed, it not having taken Lady Hammerhead and her ward long to discover that the stress at the moment in London was on simplicity. With the ready adaptation of the chameleons that they were, they had accepted the charm of the chemise dress of white muslin cut high at the waist and low at the bodice in the Grecian mode, and although Lady Hammerhead told everyone who would listen to her that muslin was being abandoned in Paris as being impractical when it was chill and damp and that taffeta, velvet and brocade were favored with necklines raised and long sleeves quite the thing,

14

she quite saw the necessity of Penelope's "fitting in," as she referred to it.

As a consequence, the two girls' dress was alike, but their demeanor was, Lady Tangle thought, quite different, Susan tending to be slightly aloof, while Penelope had chosen ceaseless vivacity as her forte. While Susan tended to take part in the various entertainments which presented themselves with a sort of distracted detachment which Lady Tangle knew meant that she was thinking of the country, Penelope was in her element, flirting right and left quite ruthlessly, much to her aunt's approval.

"Do ring for fresh tea, Dorothy," Lady Hammerhead said now with her usual petulance. "The girls will be joining us any minute, I think. I expect that Penelope is taking my advice and giving Susan a few hints as to decorum. You noticed, of course, how abrupt the poor gel was with Lord Neville when he asked her to take the floor with him at the soirée at Lady Penbrook's. Too terribly gauche!"

Lady Tangle had learned through sad experience that it would do no good to remind her friend that Lord Neville had been deep in his cups and in no condition to take the floor with anyone, and so she held her tongue. It would only annoy her to be reminded that a young and eligible Duke could do no wrong.

"I know you had no choice but to see to my coming-out, aunt," Susan had said the night before, curled at the foot of Lady Tangle's bed. "But, oh,

15

how glad I will be when all this nonsense is over and we can go back to the country."

Not wanting to encourage rebellion, Lady Tangle had said nothing. But now she was forced to admit that she wholeheartedly agreed. She hoped, of course, that the sisters would learn to be as fond of one another as they once had been, but for herself nothing could give her more pleasure than to see that last of "dear Lucinda" and the abominable Lulu.

# Chapter 2

But as soon as the girls came into the room, Lady Tangle forgot her dissatisfactions for the moment. As usual, the sight of Susan's face soothed her. The two sisters stopped for a moment just inside the door, each bending to pat their individual pet as the dogs ran to greet them. How lovely they were, Lady Tangle thought with a sudden rush of affection which included even Penelope, with their golden curls bound tight to their heads with a band of ribbon. On this occasion their gowns were identical, the white muslin flowing from their slender waists to their tiny ankles, revealing delicately slippered feet. Although she did not like to say so to Lady Hammerhead, Lady Tangle thought Penelope much improved by her choice of simpler dress.

Flushed from her brief romp with the panting Reginald, Susan hurried across the drawing room and kissed her aunt affectionately, while Penelope greeted her own guardian in a more restrained manner.

"I am sorry that we are late for tea, Aunt Dorothy," Susan declared, sitting on the footstool at Lady Tangle's feet, "but we fell to talking and forgot the time."

"Penelope had my permission to detain you, my dear," Lady Hammerhead said stiffly. "I hope that she was able to give you a few words of advice as to how to conduct yourself at Lady Winsome's soirée this evening. You really must not be so shy, you know. It does no harm for a young lady to make it clear that she is enjoying herself."

Penelope gave a little exclamation.

"Oh, but Susan has assured me that she does *not* enjoy herself and thinks it hypocritical to pretend otherwise." She smirked in the manner of one who enjoys putting others in the wrong.

"You have not represented me exactly, sister," Susan said, a spot of color appearing in both cheeks. "I said that I would behave with all due decorum but that I did not think it right to assume a false enthusiasm."

"La de da!" Lady Hammerhead exclaimed. "I expect you think that the cream of London society is not good enough for you, my girl! I expect that you find the association of country squires and their dreadful families more to your liking!"

"My dear Lucinda!" Lady Tangle protested. "There is no need for sarcasm, I think."

18

"Why, there is every need for it," Lady Hammerhead declared heatedly. "There would be every excuse for my Penelope to condescend, since she has been accustomed to an elegance you can only imagine."

Once she had started in this vein there was no stopping her, and the company was forced to hear, not for the first time, the details of a ball at Malmaison which Lady Hammerhead and her niece had attended shortly before leaving Paris.

"All the young girls wore dresses of white crêpe," she informed them, "and their hair was crowded with garlands of flowers. It was such a fine thing to see the Emperor strolling among the dancers, offering a compliment here and another there. He takes such an interest in fashion, you understand, and ladies who appear twice in the same outfit are made quite aware of his disapproval. And then, of course, the empress is so terribly chic. Not at all like that dowdy German person whom the Prince of Wales has chosen to burden himself with. It would almost be a consolation if his mistresses, at least, had any sense of style."

And, having unburdened herself temporarily, she sat even more stiffly in her chair and glared triumphantly at Lady Tangle and Susan in turn in the manner of one who has won yet another decisive battle.

"Since you think so highly of the French court, aunt, I wonder that you agreed to leave it," Susan said crisply.

Although she was always polite to her "other aunt," as she referred to her in private, Susan had long since settled in her mind the conviction that, given the opportunity, Lady Hammerhead would trample roughshod over anyone who did not make some form of protest. An independent-minded girl, Susan was unaccustomed to the verbal abuse which seemed to rise with so much readiness to the lips of Lady Hammerhead, and she was determined that a habit not be made of it, at least not in her company.

"You know that it was necessary for your sister to have her coming-out," her ladyship said sharply. "I can only hope that the gentleman she chooses to marry should share my fondness for the Continent."

"There are some who say that Napoleon will not long be contented to dictate to France alone," Susan said evenly. "There are certain policies which, were he to pursue them, would result in an alienation of his friends in this country."

"Oh, politics!" Lady Hammerhead declared. "They are matters which gentlemen discuss, but ladies do not concern themselves."

"Indeed they do not," Penelope said primly. "There is nothing which bores a gentleman more than a young lady who pretends any knowledge of politics."

"Dear Susan has so many lessons to learn," Lady Hammerhead said to Lady Tangle. "I often think that one season will not be enough to launch her."

"One season is all there will be, willy-nilly,"

Susan said firmly. "Besides, I will not have my interests dictated to by silly rules and regulations as to what I will find intriguing and what not."

"In that case, my dear, you will scarcely find yourself a husband," Lady Hammerhead declared.

"Perhaps I do not wish to find one," Susan retorted as her Aunt Dorothy flayed about helplessly with her fan.

Never had the lines of battle been more firmly drawn between her and her "other aunt," but, seeing Lady Tangle's distress, Susan hastened to change the subject.

"Shall I ring for more tea, Aunt Dorothy?" she asked.

"I have already rung, my dear," Lady Tangle said, clearly relieved at the respite.

"And that was ten minutes ago at the very least," Lady Hammerhead declared. "I believe the servants become more slovenly and useless with every passing day."

As though to substantiate her thesis, a little maid crept into the room and began a garbled apology to the effect that there had been a great to-do in the kitchen, cook having scalded herself.

"I am surprised to hear that there is anything hot enough in the kitchen to scald anyone," Lady Hammerhead said dryly.

Penelope, who found her aunt's sarcasm greatly amusing, began to titter, but Susan leaped to her feet and declared her intention of finding out how badly cook had injured herself.

"We must send for the doctor at once," Lady Tangle said in a concerned voice.

"A bit of ointment will doubtless be all that is necessary," Lady Hammerhead said sharply. "These people know how to care for themselves. Besides, it is probably only an excuse to allow cook to spend even more time resting her feet than she already does. In the meantime there must be someone belowstairs capable of making us a fresh pot of tea."

With a toss of her head, Susan followed the little maid out of the room, leaving her "other aunt" to sputter about the total impropriety of such a show of sympathy. The diatribe continued for so long that even Penelope, who took considerable enjoyment from hearing her sister criticized, began to stare into the middle distance with glazed eyes.

It came, consequently, as something of a relief when Susan returned, carrying a tray on which was set a pot of steaming tea.

"Since it seemed to mean so much to you, aunt," she said, setting the tray on the tea table, "I thought that I would make it myself."

"La, whoever heard of such a thing!" Lady Hammerhead declared.

"Cook is in considerable pain, Aunt Dorothy," Susan said, "and the doctor has been sent for. As for Rose, she was so shaken by the whole thing that I thought it wisest not to trust the tray to her."

"I cannot see why you did not let the footman serve us," Lady Hammerhead declared. "Why, I have never seen such an impulsive gel in all my life!"

"The footman was sent for the doctor, aunt," Susan replied, setting herself to pouring the tea in a competent manner.

"Duggin, then," her "other aunt" retorted, unwilling to give in even in small matters.

"Butlers do not carry tea trays." Susan said distinctly. "Poor Duggin has been criticized enough in these past weeks, and I did not see fit to give you grounds to make further complaints."

"Will you allow her to speak to you that way, Aunt Lucinda?" Penelope cried, starting to her feet.

"I will not remain in the room another minute," Lady Hammerhead declared.

Head held high, she marched out the door with Penelope following close after. The poodle, yelping plaintively, made a third.

"My dear Susan," Lady Tangle murmured. "I think this time you have gone too far."

"The best thing that could happen would be if she and my sister would find another residence," Susan said obdurately. "I am sorry, aunt. I was quite prepared to be fond of both of them and, indeed, I know I must feel a certain affection for Penelope. But it is so very difficult when both of them spend so much time criticizing and condescending."

"I fear they do not understand our ways or we theirs," Lady Tangle said sadly.

"Why, I think I understand them very well

indeed," Susan told her. "They are ambitious and grasping and they have such superficial values. Tell me, what was my sister like as a little girl? Would she have been different had she remained with you as I did?"

Speculation was not one of Lady Tangle's great strengths, and so she sat and waved her fan and her head in a distracted manner.

"I think she would have been very unhappy at Tangle Hall, even six years ago," she said finally. "Lucinda was always her favorite aunt, even when your parents were alive. There was a—a certain affinity between them."

"As there still is," Susan said thoughtfully. "And yet Papa was not like his sister, was he?"

"There never was a more sensible man," Lady Tangle said firmly.

"And Mama?" Susan said, almost fearfully.

"You are as like her as a person could be," Lady Tangle declared. "Except that dear Kate was never thoughtless."

Susan knew that that was as close as her aunt would come to a rebuke.

"I expect that I *was* rude to Aunt Lucinda," she admitted. "But when she made it so clear that she did not care what had happened to cook, I lost my temper. Still, never mind. I will apologize and that will put her in a better frame of mind, for I believe she likes apologies above anything else."

She laughed and, seating herself on the footstool again, took Lady Tangle's hand.

"I expect that I am as much a tyrant at heart as she is," she declared. "I criticize her for criticizing! How absurd everything is."

As though to express his agreement, the bulldog raised one paw and placed it in Susan's lap.

"You see," she cried, "even Reginald sees that I have been at fault!"

But even as she rubbed the dog's nose, her smile faded.

"I should like it so much if Penelope and I could come to care for one another," she said in a low voice. "Do you expect, Aunt Dorothy, that it is possible when we are so very different?"

"If you both want it so, indeed it is," Lady Tangle said gently. "But there must be an effort on both sides."

"And I shall make it," Susan declared in a decided manner. "You shall see. Tonight at the soirée I will make both Penelope and Aunt Lucinda quite proud of me."

# Chapter 3

Since Lady Winsome liked, as she put it, "the old-fashioned ways," the stylish new waltzes were never played in her ballroom. Instead the couples made their progress through cotillions which, if not less lively than the waltz, had the decided advantage, in her ladyship's eyes, of keeping hands from clasping waists for too long a period.

Penelope was inclined to raise her nose at such conservatism, declaring that no one danced anything but the waltz now in Paris; but Susan, accustomed as she was to country dances, was prepared to spend the evening quite happily twirling up and down the line. Thus it was that it was not as difficult as usual to pretend to be enjoying herself. As long as the musicians were hard at work on their instruments and there was no need for her to devote herself to the attentions of a gentleman, she could be quite content.

Her Aunt Lucinda, having accepted her apology grudgingly, had spent a considerable time that afternoon giving advice as to how Susan was to behave herself. In the first place, she was to use her fan and eyes to best advantage, being, at one and the same time, coy and flirtatious in the best Parisian fashion. When a gentleman engaged her in conversation, she was to listen to whatever he chose to say with such a degree of fascination as to make him think he was the most interesting fellow in the world. And, whatever she did, she was not to discuss politics or any other "mannish" subject. Furthermore, whenever anything amusing was said, she was to make her laughter like the tinkle of bells, thus.

At her aunt's request, Penelope had demonstrated this peculiar sound, and although Susan had not said so aloud, she had sworn to herself that never, ever would she allow such a cacophony to escape her lips.

One further outrage had been Penelope's appearance, just before they left for the ball, in a gown which was identical to the one Susan was wearing. Her aunt, she had declared, had decided that they would make even more of a sensation if they were to be dressed alike and, so they were, both in chemise dresses of light blue with the same puffed, short sleeves and the same trimming of lace at bodice and hem. Susan would have gone upstairs and changed at once had it not been that they were already late, Reginald and Lulu having engaged in a rather violent quarrel earlier which had engaged the attention of the entire household.

And so they had arrived at Lady Winsome's stately townhouse in Berkeley Square looking like mirror images of one another. Penelope and her aunt had been decidedly satisfied by the attention that had been turned on them as they had entered the ballroom, while Susan had fretted inwardly and Lady Tangle had retired, as soon as possible, to one of the gilt chairs placed along the wall and tried to fade into the background, an art at which she had become singularly adept in the past weeks.

As much to escape her mirror image as anything, Susan had accepted the first offer to dance which she had received, even though it had come from the Marquis of Ballow who fancied himself such a beau that his cravat nearly hid the lower half of his face, the upper portion being disguised, in turn, by a great mop of hair arranged in the fashionable Brutus cut. The only advantage in accepting him, outside of separating herself from Penelope, was that the cravat made it almost impossible for the gentleman to speak, while his eyes were so nearly covered by his hair as to make an exchange of meaningful looks difficult. Concentrating on his undistinguished nose, Susan had allowed herself to be led onto the floor, where she and her beau had taken their places in silence.

She could not hope for such luck during the remainder of the evening, however, and it was necessary for her to make whatever response she could to such challenging conversational gambits as the announcement that she and her sister made "a dashing fine pair." She and Penelope might as well be a pair of horses being considered for purchase at Tattersalls, she told herself and determined, in future, to send her abigail to find out what her sister was wearing before they left the house in order that she might be sure to be outfitted differently. For as long as she could remember, nearly, she had been treated as an individual, and it did not suit her at all, she found, to become, of a sudden, a curiosity in duplicate.

Still, despite her inward chafings, she knew that she was deporting herself well, although she made minimal use of her fan, not to mention her eyelashes, and would have refrained from bursting into peals of laughter, even if something had been said to even vaguely warrant it.

There were other ways in which she held her own, although she hoped her Aunt Lucinda would not notice them. That stately lady was not content to remain seated in her gilt chair, as was Lady Tangle, but marched about the ballroom, keeping a close watch on everything that happened and an eager ear open for any gossip. Seeing Lady Hammerhead's portentous progress from the vantage point of the contra line, Susan knew that they would be regaled on the way home with an assortment of scandalous tales and that that juicy main course would be followed by little driblets of compliments for Penelope and sharp bits of criticism for herself.

That was why Susan was pleased that a column intervened between herself and her Aunt Lucinda at the particular moment when Sir Edwin Gingerton attempted to become a bit more familiar than she found agreeable. A tall, gangling, red-haired fellow whose face was unpleasantly pitted by some long-past bout with the pox, he had been following her with his eyes all evening, often peering at her from an uncomfortably close distance through his peering glass. He was dressed in rather too much the pink of fashion with his evening jacket cut uncommonly high at the front and pulled apart to show a waistcoat covered with embroidered flowers of such an odd and exotic nature as to defy description.

Although she had never met Sir Edwin, Susan was all too aware of his propensities, for it was common talk among the young ladies that he was uncommonly bold and fond of saying the most outrageous and insulting intimate things in the apparently mistaken belief that they were pleasantries, not to mention compliments. As a consequence, Susan had kept well out of his way until, her current partner having gone to fetch her a glass of punch, she found that Sir Edwin had sidled up to her and was engaged in examining the area of her bodice with considerable interest and excitement.

"Miss Collins, I believe," he said in an ingratiating voice. "May I be allowed to say that . . ."

It had been at that precise point that Susan had whirled on her heel and left him, thankful that the column behind which they stood would conceal this apparent rebuff from her aunt who, doubtless, knew no more about Sir Edwin than that he was titled and eligible, an irresistible combination in her eyes no matter what a boor the gentleman might be.

So eager was Susan to get away, that she did not properly watch where she was going and found herself, quite suddenly, in a stranger's arms. Murmuring her apologies, she righted herself and drew away, only to look up into the amused, dark eyes of a gentleman she had never seen before.

"I must say that you are an extremely swift-moving young lady," he said in a low, penetrating voice, "for it was less than a moment ago that I saw you on the other side of the ballroom."

Susan could have laughed and said nothing, but, glancing over her shoulder, she saw that Sir Edwin had followed her and was, no doubt, only waiting for her to move on before accosting her again. At the same moment she saw her sister watching her from the other side of the dance floor and guessed from the expression in her eyes that she had seen the brief and disagreeable encounter which Susan had put so abruptly to an end. It gave her a shock of dismay to realize that there was nothing Penelope would have liked better than to have seen her embarrassed by Sir Edwin, and in order to prevent such an eventuality, she turned back to the stranger with some show of vivacity, explaining that the young lady he had seen at such a distance was her twin.

No sooner had she spoken than Susan was seized with an attack of resentment that she should have been forced into drawing attention to the similarity between herself and Penelope, since it was not a topic of conversation which she would normally have capitalized on. As though to mitigate her remark, she added dryly that she wondered he had not seen them together before, since they had been paraded everywhere during the past two weeks.

"I am afraid that I am rather out of things," the stranger said, looking down at her curiously, "having just returned from Italy. But, from the way you speak, I take it that you wish the similarity were not quite so exact."

It was the first time that anyone besides her Aunt Dorothy had guessed as much, and Susan looked at him in amazement.

"I believe that I can sympathize," he went on. "It must be rather difficult to be only one side of a coin."

It was put so aptly that Susan drew in her breath. But, her former companion choosing that precise moment to return with her punch, she had no recourse but to incline her head to the stranger and move away.

Lord Owens was a pleasant enough fellow who shared Susan's love of dancing, and she had been his partner twice that evening and several times before at other entertainments and it only followed, given his open nature, that he should make some comment.

" 'Pon my soul," he exclaimed, "so you know the viscount, do you?"

Giving in to her curiosity, Susan asked why that should be so extraordinary, adding as she did that she had never been introduced to the gentleman in question and had only passed a moment of casual conversation with him. And, even as she spoke the words, she acknowledged to herself that, in some peculiar way, there had been nothing casual at all about what she and the stranger had said to one another in those few brief moments.

Seemingly eager to inform, Lord Owens had told her that the viscount was Lord Powell and that he had only expressed surprise at thinking she might know him because the gentleman did not make a habit of extending his acquaintance to very young ladies.

"I believe he prefers the company of a few close friends and is inclined to find such soirées as this quite frivolous," Lord Owens went on. "A curious fellow, that. A serious turn of mind, they say, and not one to haunt the gaming tables and the ballrooms."

"If that is the case," Susan replied, sipping her punch and assuming a casual air to hide the fact that she was very much intrigued, "what is he doing here, pray?"

Lord Owens pursed his lips. "I believe he has a younger sister who is having her coming-out," he

34

said. "The mother is a bit of an invalid, I think, and, no doubt, finds constant attendance at such affairs too arduous."

His eyes lit up as the music began again, and relieving Susan of her glass which he engagingly placed in a potted fern, he offered her his arm. And, even knowing as she did that her Aunt Lucinda would be annoyed that she had danced so often with a young gentleman whose father had left him with an estate vastly encumbered with debt, Susan gladly took her place on the dance floor opposite him.

And so the evening went pleasantly enough and Susan was able to forget the slight unpleasantness which Sir Edwin had caused. She did not forget her conversation with Lord Powell, however, and it was with some considerable pleasure, not to mention surprise, that she encountered him later, on which occasion he asked her if she would go in to supper with him.

"But we have not even been introduced yet, sir," Susan murmured.

"I confess to having made a few inquiries," he told her, his dark eyes intent on hers. "You are Miss Susan Collins, I believe."

"And you are Lord Powell," she replied, laughing. "You see, I have made inquiries of my own, although, no doubt, it is indelicate of me to admit it."

"I would rather call it honesty," he replied.

And so it was decided that they would sup together in the large dining room downstairs where,

Lord Powell assured her, there was certain to be a lavish spread, Lady Winsome fancying herself a hostess of the first water.

Susan had no more than taken his arm, however, when a tiny, dark elf of a girl hurried up to him and expressed a desire to speak to him for a moment privately.

"Miss Collins, let me introduce my sister Evelyn," Lord Powell said with an indulgent smile for the tiny creature. "Will you excuse us for a moment?"

Susan assured him that she would and watched Evelyn draw him into an alcove where she whispered something to him excitedly, some trivia, no doubt, about a new beau.

How pleasant it would be, she thought, to have a supper companion with whom she could truly talk. As other couples bustled past her on their way to the stairs, she stood lost in thought until someone took her arm roughly. Looking up, she saw Sir Edwin Gingerton grinning at her foolishly.

" 'Pon my soul I thought I would never find you in the crush," he announced. "Let's be off now or there'll be no more of the smoked salmon left."

"I cannot think what you are talking of," Susan declared in an outraged voice. "I have made arrangements to take supper with someone else, sir, and you will be good enough to let go of my arm!"

"Why, what a jade you are!" Sir Edwin announced in a shrill voice. "Not more than half an hour ago you were rolling your eyes at me and telling me that nothing would give you more pleasure than to be my companion at the table."

"What's this, now?" Susan heard Lord Powell protest. Clearly he had overheard what Sir Edwin had called her and his dark eyes glittered. Over his shoulder, Susan saw his sister going off happily with a young gentleman who was looking down at her fondly.

"Why, the gel's a flirt, that's what!" Sir Edwin replied, not loosening his hold on Susan's arm. "She gave her word, sir, and I am not prepared to be made a fool of!"

"If that is the case, I would lower my voice," Lord Powell said with an ominous note in his voice. "We are attracting some attention, and I am sure that is not to the lady's liking."

"She should have thought of that when she made such a play for me earlier," Sir Edwin declared.

"But I did no such thing!" Susan protested with some considerable energy. "When you accosted me over there by the column, I walked away from you, if you recall."

"Ah, but later you had a change of heart," Sir Edwin announced. "Standing just there by that window, you flirted with me for all you were worth and said that you would be delighted to sup with me."

"I saw the episode you are referring to, sir," Lord Powell said grimly. "Miss Susan Collins was dancing at the time. It was her sister you were talking to."

"Impossible!" Sir Edwin cried in his disagreeably

high voice. "Why, she told me herself that her name was Susan and that, when no one was listening, I should feel quite free to call her by it."

A sudden comprehension swept over Susan and she shivered. At the same moment, Lord Powell took Sir Edwin by the shoulder and propelled him to one side. There followed a conversation from which Sir Edwin emerged with a hangdog look. Murmuring something which might or might not have been an apology to Susan, he slunk away.

"And so," Lord Powell said in a low voice, returning to Susan's side, "what are we to make of that?"

It was clear that he was very angry, although now that Sir Edwin had been sent on his way, he was bent on controlling himself.

"It seems," he went on, "that your twin sister has played a singularly unpleasant trick on you."

"It seems she has," Susan whispered, half speaking to herself.

Something inside her seemed to have shriveled and died.

"Would you like to talk about it," Lord Powell said gently.

"Not now," she told him. "I do not think I could bear even to think of it just now."

"Then we will speak of other things," he assured her, taking her arm. "Trust me to distract you, Miss Collins. Of all things, it would give me the greatest pleasure."

# Chapter 4

That night, being driven home in the lozenged coach which she and her Aunt Dorothy had brought down from the country, Susan was very quiet, and so, surprisingly enough, were the others. Usually, after a ball, Lady Hammerhead was full of gossip, but tonight she was only an ominous shadow on the leather seat opposite. Lady Tangle, who usually offered a few timid pleasantries about the evening, satisfied herself with gripping Susan's gloved hand with her own, and Penelope uttered not a word.

Susan was glad enough of the absence of conversation. During supper Lord Powell, true to his word, had attempted to distract her from what he, no doubt, guessed would be disquieting thoughts by speaking of Italy and the glories of Florence and Rome. And Susan had listened intently, making intelligent comments when she could, while the back of her mind whirled with the knowledge that her sister could have attempted to play such a cruel joke on her.

Now, with a thin rain pelting against the carriage top, she could no longer avoid asking the question, why. If Lord Powell had not been there to protect her, a terrible scene might have ensued when Sir Edwin had accosted her, for, on no account, would she have agreed to accompany him down to supper. Remembering how loudly his thin voice had been pitched, she shuddered. He had called her a jade and said that she had deliberately led him on. If Lord Powell had not cut him short, there was no knowing what he would have declared in his anger. He was no gentleman and he did not know how to treat a lady as such. Doubtlessly a crowd would have collected around them, and the scene would have made a scandal which would have been repeated in every drawing room in London by the next afternoon.

Why should Penelope have wished to see her so embarrassed, Susan asked herself. Could it be that her sister had seen her in conversation with Lord Powell earlier and devised the trick to provide her with some relief for her pique at seeing her sister with the most sought-after gentleman in the room? For Susan was certain that Lord Powell was no less than that. Certainly Lord Owens had hinted at it, and any additional proof she might have required had been provided by the envious glances shot in her direction when she had entered the dining room on his arm.

Still, whatever Penelope's motive, what she had done had been not only unfair but dreadfully unkind. Until now Susan had thought that she and her sister only needed time to acquaint one another with their ways, but matters were, it seemed, more complex than that. Penelope had treated her as though she were an enemy, and the thought filled Susan with anxiety and consternation. Was Penelope quiet now because she knew that Susan had realized what was behind Sir Edwin's demands? Or was it simple annoyance that Susan had supped with the most handsome gentleman at the ball while she herself had been forced to be content with a middle-aged marquis who had paid far more attention to the sweetmeats and oyster patties than he had to her?

As for what ailed her Aunt Lucinda, Susan was to find out soon enough, for as soon as they had reached the house in Grosvenor Square, Lady Hammerhead had indicated in an abrupt manner that she would be obliged if they would join her in the sitting room for a glass of ratafia before they all retired.

This in itself was enough to set Susan's already unsteady nerves on edge, since her "other aunt" was in the habit of hurrying everyone off to bed, the girls particularly, for the reason that they might appear at their best the next day. And, although she had a certain fondness for wine herself, Lady Ham-

41

merhead often said that it would ruin a gel's complexion. Now, however, once the glasses had been handed round, she cleared her throat ominously.

Susan's first thought when they had been ordered to the sitting room was to refuse. In the first place, she was not certain she could trust herself if she was forced to speak to Penelope that evening. Added to this was the fact that she sensed that some unpleasantness was in the air, and she thought—indeed she was certain—that she had had enough of that for one day. But, on the other hand, she did not wish her Aunt Dorothy to be subjected without protection, to whatever it was that Lady Hammerhead had to say. Besides it was clear that something was on both the older ladies' minds, and Susan guessed that whatever it was must be aired to her and Penelope together.

"You did yourself very well tonight, Susan," Lady Hammerhead began grudgingly. "I made it my business to make inquiries about the gentleman with whom you supped, and it seems that his—er, credentials could not be higher."

In the candlelight, her turban, topped as it was with an ostrich feather, cast a grotesque shadow on the wall behind her chair. Although she offered congratulations, her face was sharper than usual, her expression even more disapproving. In the chair opposite her aunt, Penelope stared at her fingers, which were busy knotting and unknotting the fringe of her cashmere shawl.

"It seems that Lord Powell has several large estates in the country, not to mention an elegant townhouse," Lady Hammerhead went on as grimly as though she were reciting an obituary notice. "No one with whom I spoke had anything but praise for him, although, I take it, he is fond of keeping himself to himself, particularly when young ladies are concerned. You were very clever to entice him as you did."

"I did not entice him, aunt," Susan said in a clear, even voice. "We enjoyed a pleasant conversation over supper. There was nothing more to it than that."

"This is not the time for disclaimers, my dear," Lady Hammerhead said dryly. "No doubt you think that by making light of it you will make your—your conquest more amazing still."

"There was no conquest, aunt," Susan said flatly and left it at that, having seen from the contortions of her Aunt Dorothy's face that that gentle-hearted lady feared a quarrel of the sort that had erupted that afternoon.

Lady Hammerhead bent forward in her chair.

"Do you mean to say," she demanded, "that Lord Powell made no arrangements to see you again?"

Susan considered carefully before she answered and made no pretense at doing otherwise. It was true that Lord Powell had made no suggestion of a formal visit to the house on Grosvenor Square, but in the process of their conversation, he had determined that she rode every morning in the park at the unfashionable hour of nine, and she had noted that he had taken pains to ask if her sister accompanied her. Since Penelope was no horsewoman, Susan had been able to reply that she rode alone. Nothing more had been said on the subject, and as consequence, she decided that she could truthfully inform her "other aunt" that no plans for another meeting had been made.

Still, she resented the tone of this interrogation and determined to end it as soon as possible. Whatever it was her Aunt Dorothy had to say—and she was certain it was something—clearly had nothing to do with Lord Powell, since during this discussion, she had continued to wear a distracted air.

"In that case, there is no more to say on that particular matter," Lady Hammerhead said firmly. "No doubt Lord Powell was distracting himself for the evening only."

It was clear from the way she spoke that she hoped that was the case, at least as far as Susan was concerned.

"Besides," that formidable lady went on, "we have more important business to discuss. Penelope, do stop fidgeting with that shawl and look at me!"

Never before had Susan heard Lady Hammerhead speak in such sharp tones to her sister, and she knew that it must be because, for that evening at least, Penelope had been outshone. It occurred to her that, amazing as it might seem, her Aunt Lucinda knew something of the trick Penelope had played and was about to rebuke her. But it became immediately apparent that such was not the case.

"Dorothy and I have had a communication," Lady Hammerhead went on in a rasping voice. "It only arrived as we were leaving, and I did not have occasion to read it until we reached Lady Winsome's. It is my decision that the sooner both of you gels know of the contents of the letter the better, since it will change one of your lives completely."

"I do think, Lucinda, that it would be better left till tomorrow," Lady Tangle said in a troubled voice. Casting her an anxious look, Susan saw that her aunt's face was pale and her expression forlorn.

"Then let us leave it till then," Susan said, rising from her chair and setting the untouched glass of ratafia on the table beside her. "There was never any news which could not wait."

"As usual, you take too much on you, Susan," Lady Hammerhead snapped. "I should have thought you would have taught her better, Dorothy. Certain decisions are for adults to make and this is one of them."

Susan was about to protest that her aunt was an adult and that it was clearly her choice not to undertake this disclosure, whatever it might be, at this particular time, but Lady Tangle cast her such an imploring look that she sank back onto her chair, noticing how studiously Penelope avoided looking at her. She determined that tomorrow they would have the matter of Sir Edwin out when they were alone together, to clear the air between them, if nothing else. How unlike life in the country this all was, she thought with a wave of dismay, with quarrels to settle and important communications to impart. She yearned for the day when the season would be over and she and her aunt could return to Somerset.

"The message was from your granduncle, Lord Failfoot," Lady Hammerhead said eyeing both girls in turn. "You know of his existence, I believe."

Susan communicated her bewilderment to her Aunt Dorothy with a puzzled glance. She did, indeed, know something of her granduncle, and what she knew made it difficult for her to believe that he had written a letter to any member of the family, since the elderly earl had kept himself cut off from his family for years, apparently content to live the life of a misanthrope in a decaying mansion in Yorkshire. Her Aunt Dorothy had often told her that the poor gentleman was much to be pitied, but she had never given any details as to when or why he had become so unpleasantly eccentric.

"Why, of course, I know of his existence, aunt," Penelope declared, rousing herself. "You know that, at your urging, I have written him once every Christmas, although he has never had the good grace to make a reply. You have often told me that since he is so very wealthy and has no heir . . ."

"Yes, yes," her aunt interrupted her impatiently. "There is no need to go into all of that, my dear. The important thing is that he has written to an-

46

nounce that he will join us in London immediately. Indeed, there is every likelihood that he will arrive tomorrow, since the letter was delayed. That is why I thought it imperative that you should know of it tonight."

"He intends to join us!" Susan exclaimed. "But is it not true, Aunt Dorothy, that he has not left Yorkshire for the past thirty years, at least?"

"That is quite so, my dear," Lady Tangle murmured. "This is such shocking news that, I assure you, it has put me in a twitter. I only met him once when I was only a girl myself and, although I would not like to say that he was unpleasant . . ."

"He is very unpleasant indeed," Lady Hammerhead interrupted. "One must call a spade a spade. But he is also rich as Croesus and, as Penelope says, he has no heir. One must be prepared to put up with a great deal but for a purpose."

"What purpose, aunt?" Penelope said excitedly, all of her former sulkiness having disappeared.

"He writes to say that, since he cannot live forever and since it has always been his firm belief that fortunes should not only remain in a family but be left undivided, he has managed to overcome his reluctance to make any member of the opposite sex wealthy," Lady Hammerhead said triumphantly. "Those are his precise words."

"But what has that to do with us?" Susan demanded. "He cannot mean . . ."

"That is precisely what he does mean, my dear," Lady Hammerhead said stiffly. "One of you two

47

gels will inherit. It is as simple as that. He only needs to observe you, as he puts it, to come to a decision."

Penelope so far forgot herself as to clap her hands, but Susan whirled to her feet angrily.

"I do not wish to be observed!" she exclaimed. "I will tell him at once that I want to be part of no— no contest for his money!"

Lady Hammerhead shrugged her shoulders.

"As for that," she said, "you must do as you see fit. But I must warn you that, old as he is, he has kept a quite terrible temper." She cleared her voice. "I have made a point of keeping in touch with his housekeeper," she said in a low voice, "and so, you see, I know something of what to expect."

"Temper he may have," Susan declared, "but that is no reason that we should be subjected to it."

Lady Tangle laid a soothing hand on her arm.

"There is this to consider, my dear," she said. "You know I have no more thought for his wealth than you have, but he is a very old gentleman and perhaps, as the end draws near, he feels the need to have some family about him, no matter how distant. And, besides, in his own peculiar way, he was as fond of your and Penelope's father as he ever was of anyone. Given that, it can do no harm to be cordial to him."

Susan flushed, ashamed of her own impetuousness. Too much had happened today. She could not take it in properly. She only knew that she would not compete for an old man's money.

"Well, as for that," she murmured, "I will be pleasant to him."

"Oh, I expect you will," Penelope mocked her. "For all your fine protests, you would be as glad as anyone to be an heiress, wouldn't you?"

The hurt Susan felt was almost too much to bear. Slowly she went to stand beside her sister's chair.

"Why do you hate me so much?" she said in a low voice. And then, without waiting for an answer, fled the room.

# Chapter 5

Although Lord Failfoot's arrival was known to be imminent, it was scarcely to be expected that the eccentric old gentleman would make his appearance at the house on Grosvenor Square at ten the next morning, having spent the night at an inn just outside London and rising before the sun to make his descent on an already disquieted household.

Lady Hammerhead made the announcement, dragging Penelope behind her to Susan's bedchamber.

"Thank heaven you are already dressed," she told the girl, dismissing Susan's abigail with a glance. "He is even more dreadful than I remembered him. Fancy anyone demanding claret at this time in the morning and he with one foot swollen with the gout! He has installed himself in the drawing room and demands to see both of you gels at once!"

"Then he must be disappointed," Susan said with a calmness she did not feel, "for, as you see, I have not yet attended to my hair."

"Penelope will help you," Lady Hammerhead declared, pushing her niece into the room. "I must repair to the drawing room at once, since Dorothy is in such a twitter that she may put him off."

Susan only hoped that someone would. Having received word from her abigail that cook was keeping to her bed, she did not know what possible arrangements could be made to provide meals for what promised to be a most demanding visitor. She had also been piqued, on rising at eight, to see that a heavy rain would keep her from her customary ride in the park. Although not for one moment expecting to find Lord Powell waiting for her there, she was, however, aware of being unusually disappointed at being kept inside.

And now, to add to the general confusion, she must share the burden of entertaining a granduncle whom she had never met and whose ideas as to inheritance appalled her. She realized, as Lady Hammerhead shut the door behind her, that there was also to be the nuisance of being alone with Penelope for the first time since the trick involving Sir Edwin Gingerton had been played on her.

"Well, we are for it, I see," Susan said, picking up her brush and seating herself at the vanity table before the window. "And sooner than we had expected."

"He is only a crotchety old man," Penelope said suddenly, avoiding Susan's eyes.

"Anyone who wishes to control the destiny of one of us is something more than that," Susan said in a low voice, brushing her curls so vehemently that they stood out around her head like a burst of sunshine. At the same time she was busy noting in the mirror that Penelope had chosen to wear one of her Parisian frocks in a clear attempt to distinguish herself. Obviously she had no intention of being confused with her twin on this first meeting with the gentleman who might, in a stroke, make her a wealthy woman.

"La, you *are* in a temper, aren't you?" Penelope said, flouncing down on the edge of the four-posted bed. "I would go down without you if it were not that it is Aunt Lucinda's express wish that we should make our usual joint appearance."

For the first time it occurred to Susan that, after the original sensation caused by their appearance together in London, their similarity might give her sister as much cause for annoyance as it did her. The idea made her just sympathetic enough to feel that she could safely introduce the subject of Sir Edwin.

"Why did you do it?" she said, turning on the stool.

Penelope had the good grace to pretend confusion.

"Indeed," she said, "I do not know what you are speaking of. Besides, there is no time for idle chatter. They are expecting us downstairs."

"There is something to settle between us first," Susan said firmly. "Let me say that I know, as well as you, how difficult all of this has been. We have been raised in different worlds and then, quite suddenly been shunted together. Sisters and strangers both at the same time. It is only to be expected that there should be certain stresses. And yet I cannot understand . . ."

"And if there have," Penelope interrupted almost defiantly, "this is no time to speak of it. We must turn all of our attention to our granduncle."

"If we are to deal with him," Susan said in a low voice, "we must first know what to expect from one another. I thought, until last evening, that you were prepared to be, at least, a friend to me."

"We are sisters," Penelope said sharply, as though confronted with a paradox. "What has friendship to do with it?"

But Susan was not prepared to be put off so easily.

"You will remember that last night I asked you why you hated me," she murmured.

"It was a strange thing to say," Penelope said crossly. "Aunt Lucinda *would* ask me why and I told her that I thought the ratafia had gone to your head."

"Since I did not so much as taste it, that is scarcely a possibility," Susan told her. "I think you

54

knew well enough that I was referring to the awkward situation you placed me in with Lord Edwin."

"I?" Penelope exclaimed. "Why, I have not the slightest idea what you are talking about except that the gentleman is the most frightful sort of boor."

"And yet, despite that, you took the opportunity to flirt with him most outrageously," Susan said, her eyes steady on her sister's face.

Penelope made as though to protest, but Susan did not wait to give her the opportunity to lie. Indeed, she dreaded that possibility, constituting, as it would, the final outrage.

"Lord Powell saw you with Sir Edwin earlier in the evening," she told her sister. "He described your behavior and that, together with Sir Edwin's assurance that he had engaged Miss Susan Collins for supper, made your scheme quite clear. Oh, Penelope, why did you do it?"

Rising from the bed, her twin went to the pier glass in the corner and made a pretext of arranging the lace collar of her rather elaborate morning dress. She mumbled something that Susan could not hear.

After a pause, Susan went to stand behind her. At once Penelope lowered her eyes, but Susan lifted her chin with gentle fingers until they were staring straight at one another in the glass, double mirror images and yet with such a difference between them that Susan thought only they could detect.

"It—it was an impulse," Penelope said, jerking her chin away. "A little joke."

"Not a very pleasant joke," Susan murmured. "As you must have guessed, Sir Edwin made rather a scene. He called me a jade. Is that what you wanted?"

"You are so—so full of yourself!" Penelope exclaimed, whirling to face her sister. "So self-righteous and condescending. All of this is quite beneath you, isn't it? You make me out to be a calculating fortune hunter and you clearly despise Aunt Lucinda. *We* have been contaminated by Continental airs. But you are the proper English virgin with all your talk of horses and the country!"

Susan stared at her, amazed. How differently they each saw the situation. It had never occurred to her that she might appear to condescend. And if she spoke of riding and Somerset, she only did so because they were her loves. But, of course, they were no more dear to her than Paris and high society were to Penelope. Neither of them could escape their upbringing. It seemed quite terrible to her that she had not realized that before.

"I am sorry if that is how you see me," she murmured, holding out her arms.

Penelope's face was flushed and her lower lip was crimson where she had bitten it.

"We *shall* be fond of one another," Susan promised her.

And yet, even when they embraced, there was the nagging thought that no matter how much her sister irritated her, she would never have stooped to playing such a cruel trick on her. Closing her eyes, with Penelope's soft cheek against hers, Susan reminded herself that, perhaps, in Paris, such displays of spite were common enough not to have allowed her sister to discriminate against them.

Thus it was, a temporary peace having been made, that they descended the stairs together and entered the drawing room. The scene which met their eyes there was not reassuring.

A bright fire was blazing in the fireplace, and beside it in the Chippendale wing chair sat a wizened old man slouched low against the cushions which had been placed behind his back, one leg elevated on still more cushions which had been piled on a footstool. He was wearing an old-fashioned powdered periwig, and his face was like a wrinkled apple kept too long in the bin. His clothing was that of a generation past, and his short pantaloons ended at the knees, displaying swollen white-stockinged legs. He held an ear trumpet of magnificent proportions in one hand and, in the other, a cane with which he beat time in tune to some melody or other heard only by him, the tempo of which was apparently very fast indeed.

Across from him, Lady Tangle gave the impression of huddling on the sofa, while Lady Hammerhead, who was standing by his side, bent to bellow in his ear trumpet: "Here are the gels, my lord!"

As she and Penelope walked toward the old

gentleman, Susan saw that there was nothing aged about her granduncle's eyes. Indeed, they seemed to penetrate hers before passing on to Penelope.

"A bit of nonsense, this!" Lord Failfoot roared in a voice which would have done credit to a bargeman. The effect of such a noise coming from one who looked so frail was utterly disconcerting, although Susan told herself that, no doubt, it was a result of his apparent deafness. Even so, she was in some doubt as to how to respond to his singular pronouncement. Did he mean that his being here was nonsense? If so, she was inclined to agree.

But, if Susan hesitated, Penelope did not. Darting toward the old gentleman in her most graceful manner, she bent and planted a kiss on his wrinkled forehead, whereupon Lord Failfoot began to beat about her with his cane with such effect that she made as rapid a retreat as her advance had been.

"That is Penelope, sir," Lady Hammerhead said with an unusual tentative note in her voice. "You will recall that *she* always writes to you at Christmas. Indeed, as my ward . . ."

"Can't hear a word you say!" the old gentleman declared. "What's your name, gel? Come along. Speak up?"

Since he was training his eyes on her, Susan knew that she must make a reply, although she had no intention of going close enough to him to risk being struck by the ubiquitous cane.

"I am Susan, sir," she said in her ordinary voice.

"Susan, eh?" he said. "Excellent enunciation! No

58

one speaks clearly these days, you know! Great thing to find someone who knows how to move her mouth. First credits go to you, chit! First credits!"

Lady Hammerhead seemed to expand with annoyance.

"Perhaps, sir," she said, taking the liberty of placing his ear trumpet to his ear, "if you would use this, you could hear us all quite clearly."

Lord Failfoot flung the offending article to the floor.

"Never use the damned thing when there's someone in the room I can hear without it!" he exclaimed. "Come sit beside me, chit, and explain why I should have been given this sour claret. A fine welcome! I should have brought my own stock if I had known there was no proper cellar in this blasted place."

Susan had been prepared to be annoyed by this unknown and uninvited relative, but she was surprised to find herself, instead, amused. Clearly her granduncle had nurtured rudeness to a fine art and, if nothing more than that was expected of him, there could be no surprises. He was prepared, obviously, to be impossible, and she determined to let nothing stand in his path.

"If the wine is sour, sir," she said, taking the chair beside him, "we will send for another bottle and hope for the best."

The notion seemed to amuse him, for he broke into a rusty laugh which ended in a fit of choking. A pale string of a manservant whom Susan had not noticed materialized to clap his master on the back, only to be rewarded by a stroke of the cane which struck him on the shoulder.

"Do as the gel said, Brattle!" Lord Failfoot roared. "Fetch another bottle and be quick about it!"

The valet hurried from the room, nursing his shoulder with one hand. And, at the same time, Susan, with quiet deliberateness, removed the cane from her granduncle's grip.

"Eh, what's that then!" Lord Failfoot cried. "What do you think you are doing, gel?"

"Protecting myself, sir," Susan said calmly. "I think you have too good an aim."

"Can't hear! Can't hear!" he bellowed. "Well, never mind. Where's my man got to?"

"He's gone to fetch another bottle of claret, sir!" Lady Hammerhead cried in a mighty voice.

"Damme, don't shout at me, woman!" Lord Failfoot shouted in return. "Stubble it!"

At this quaintly phrased suggestion that she shut up, Lady Hammerhead colored a dingy scarlet.

"The man is even more impossible than I thought he might be," she said to Penelope in a low voice. "It is not enough that he is eccentric, but he must be senile and deaf as well. How strange it is that his housekeeper did not mention that he had lost his hearing. If we had only known, my dear, we might have provided you with elocution lessons, although why he praises Susan for her enunciation, I cannot tell."

The valet chose this moment to return to the room, carrying a silver tray crowned with a bottle. Lord Failfoot indicated his approval by rubbing his hands together and muttering to himself under his breath as his man attended to serving him.

"Fancy!" Lady Hammerhead went on, this time including Lady Tangle and Susan in her audience, although she kept her voice low. "Fancy, drinking claret at this hour of the morning and he with gout! But expect that we must let him indulge himself. Indeed, it is probably quite the best thing."

The implication that the sooner the old man died the better was quite clear, and Susan wondered if her Aunt Lucinda took a special pleasure in saying as much directly in front of him, albeit with her back turned so that there was no chance that he would read her lips.

"My dear Lucinda," Lady Tangle said in a troubled voice. "I really do not think that you should say such things, since I am certain that you do not mean them."

"Talk away! Talk away!" Lord Failfoot roared, draining his glass. "No need to pay any attention to an old muckworm like me. Make it clear I'm not wanted. Very well! Very well! I can always leave my fortune to some slip-gibbeted charity or other."

Lady Hammerhead whirled about to shed the rays of a brilliant smile on him while out of the corner of her mouth urging Penelope to do the same.

"Damme, that's better!" the old man declared. "Doesn't matter whether you mean it, of course. No one *means* anything. World's a cage of hypocrites! That's why I've stayed out of it these many years. Thought everything might have changed, but might have known better. There's no length anyone won't go if there's money to be had. Come along, gel! What are you frowning at?"

Susan started to speak and then remembered how, in the bedchamber upstairs, Penelope had accused her of being self-satisfied and condescending, as though she were better than anyone else, more upright, more honest. If she were to tell her grand-uncle what she thought of his general condemnation of mankind, she would, she knew, only succeed in sounding smug. Besides, perhaps in a general way, he was right. Even she was a hypocrite for being in this room. Very well, if he wanted her to smile, she would smile and have done with it.

"That's better!" Lord Failfoot announced, his dark eyes darting from face to face. "Now, I suppose these gels have been told what I propose to do for one of them. No need to make a nuisance of yourself with any twaddle. Nod if it's yes and shake the head if it's no. Have you told them or haven't you?"

Lady Hammerhead and Lady Tangle nodded their heads in unison, the latter with such an expression of terror on her face that Susan wanted to lead her out of the room. She wondered if her aunt were having second thoughts about the need to be sympathetic and understanding to an old and, perhaps, dying man.

"And what did they think of the idea, eh?" Lord Failfoot demanded.

Penelope smiled more broadly still, but the charade was too disgraceful for Susan to continue.

"I think it is a dreadful scheme," she said, speaking slowly and clearly, "and I intend to have no part in any competition with my sister."

"Couldn't hear a word you said!" Lord Failfoot said triumphantly. "By the look of you, you think a little protest is in order. Want it all yourself without any to-do. Gels were the same in my day. Sly money-mongers, all of them."

It occurred to Susan that even though he was her granduncle, and old and deaf to boot, she would not be spoken to that way. In the process of rising to take her departure, she happened to dislodge a book of poems by Blake which she had been reading the day before from the table on which she had left it, the table which separated her and her granduncle's chairs.

The book struck the carpeted floor with a dull thud which the other three ladies, rapt with horror at the browbeating they were receiving, did not appear to hear. But, at the sound, muted though it was, Lord Failfoot jumped a little in his chair, causing his gouty leg to twitch. And yet he was not even holding his trumpet to his ear!

Susan stared at him with dawning realization of the truth, which was, quite certainly, that this rude, old gentleman who was continuing his diatribe with such vigor was not deaf at all. On the contrary, if he heard the book fall, he must have very penetrating hearing indeed.

Slipping back onto her chair, Susan clenched her hands tight together, not certain whether to be amused or angry. What a rapscallion the old man was, to be sure. And how he must have laughed to himself when Lady Hammerhead had made those indiscreet comments about him. How fortunate for Penelope that she had not contributed her own impressions of her granduncle.

Still, the old man must not be allowed to continue to deceive them. And yet how was she to expose him? If she were to accost him with the truth, he would only deny it or bellow the louder. Either that or pretend not to hear her as he had done when she had told him, a few moments before, that she did not intend to compete with her sister for his fortune.

He had, she noted, worked himself into a fair passion now, beating the arm of his chair with a wrinkled old fist and shaking his ear trumpet with the other. The subject on which he had now embarked seemed to be the corruption of the *beau monde* where nothing was done properly any longer.

Quickly Susan slipped out of her chair and went to stand behind his. No one seemed to notice. The old man roared and growled to his heart's content, while the three ladies before him visibly wilted before his eyes. Only the valet, discreetly standing in the alcove by the window, stared at Susan curiously.

She had to wait some time for it, but the moment arrived at last in which Lord Failfoot was forced to pause to take a breath and in that moment of silence Susan spoke in a clear, low voice.

"I believe I smell smoke," she said. "I think the house must be on fire."

Since she was standing behind her granduncle, there was no way he could read her lips. And certainly she had not spoken loudly enough to be heard even by someone who was moderately hard of hearing. How strange it was then that her pronouncement should have had such an effect.

"Fire?" Lord Failfoot exclaimed. "Fire! Damme, someone hand me my cane. Give me a hand, Brattle. Out of the way, all of you! Out of the way!"

Half-supported by his valet, Lord Failfoot picked up an amazing speed by the time he was halfway across the room. In a moment he had disappeared into the hall, and a moment after that, the front door was heard to slam behind him.

"But I cannot smell the least sign of smoke, my dear," Lady Tangle said.

"You must have imagined it," Penelope said with a frown. "If this shock should do our granduncle any harm, you shall have to take the blame for it."

"Don't you see the favor Susan has done us, sapskull?" Lady Hammerhead said, addressing her niece with unaccustomed vehemence. "The old gudgeon is no more deaf than I am. All that nonsense about not being able to hear was just a Banbury story. He could pretend not to hear anything he didn't want to be told!"

"And he could listen to people talk about him in a low voice," Susan murmured. "As long as we thought he couldn't hear . . ."

Lady Hammerhead's sharp-nosed face grew a dead white.

"Oh, dear, oh, dear," she wailed. "I expect he overheard it all. Every word. Tell me, Penelope, precisely what was it I said? Oh, my dear, I am so glad you had the wit not to agree with me."

While she babbled on, Lady Tangle reached out her hand to Susan.

"I expect that he deserved to be exposed," she said. "But it will make things very awkward. Very awkward, indeed. I do not think he is the sort of gentleman who likes to eat humble pie."

"Very well," Susan said thoughtfully. "I will see that he does not. There must be a way. There always is. But, for the present, I think it will be enough for Duggin to take out the message that I was mistaken about smelling smoke. After all, it will do the old gentleman no good to stand about in the street. Indeed, I am certain all of this confusion must have tired him."

"I see your drift, my dear," Lady Tangle said approvingly. "We will go our separate ways and Duggin will show his lordship to his room."

"And the next time we all have occasion to meet," Susan said, "no mention will be made to the absence of the ear trumpet. We will speak normally and there will be no attempt to accommodate his so-called deafness. If he is the sort of old-fashioned aristocrat I think he is, he will follow the adage: 'Never apologize. Never explain.' And, if he does, we can put this sort of nonsense behind us."

# Chapter 6

As it turned out, although it was true that the ear trumpet never made another appearance and no further mention was made of auditory affliction, the old gentleman continued to make a specialty of nonsense of the most annoying sort. One could give him credit for originality at least, Susan thought, for surely there were not many people who "got their blood going" in the morning by virtue of consuming a bumper of brandy on rising, with the result that he sat down to breakfast in a slightly tipsy mood which resulted in a few embarrassments such as his mistaking the salt for sugar and Lady Hammerhead for the footman.

There were other annoying idiosyncrasies, as well, such as his lordship's propensity for pinching the maids with a vigorousness which would have done credit to a man half his age. He also developed a fondness for baiting the two dogs against one another with the result that Lulu, being no match for the hulking Reginald, spent a good deal of her time cowering in corners and yelping hysterically. Easily bored, Lord Failfoot was happiest when there was excitement of some sort and quickly found that the best way to produce it was to fabricate any sort of tale which would set the two older ladies at odds. He was constantly to be found whispering stories to one or the other of them. Lady Tangle, in tears, reported to Susan that he had told her that Lady Hammerhead had told him that, because of "dear Dorothy's" doltishness, there were many houses at which they were no longer welcome. Lady Hammerhead, on the other hand, raged about for days on the basis of the old man having assured her that Lady Tangle thought that half the stories she told about her experiences in Paris were so many lies.

Meanwhile Penelope smiled until her face seemed about to crack and would not let half an hour pass without asking her granduncle if there was not something she could do for him. In this she showed considerable perseverance, since his usual response was to either tell her to get away or, if a favor could be done him, to call her Susan. Actually Susan was certain that he had been able to identify one of them from the other early on and that he never called one by the other's name unless it would serve the purpose of annoying them.

Meanwhile, she set herself in the role of

peacekeeper, wiping away Lady Tangle's tears and soothing Lady Hammerhead with the reminder that he was a very old man indeed.

"Oh, but he is vicious," the latter would often say in a low voice, as though speaking to herself. "Fancy his pretending to be deaf the way he did! And, as for his plan of making either you or Penelope his heiress, I cannot think how he can make a proper decision when he absolutely refuses to listen to me on the subject. Sitting here in the house all day, how can he be a judge of your performances in public? And yet when I suggested that we hold a soirée here for his benefit, he absolutely refused to hear of it. Indeed, I never thought to hear such language uttered by a gentleman in my presence!"

Susan was forced to agree that her granduncle's language was colorful in the extreme, since he had a fondness for old-fashioned slang and vulgarisms, many of which, perhaps fortunately, she did not understand. But she assumed the air of one who is impossible to shock in which she simply emulated the attitude of the unflappable Brattle.

For three days after her granduncle's arrival Susan was kept from riding because of the continuing bad weather, and when finally, one morning, she awoke to find the sun shining, nothing could have kept her from her nine o'clock canter in the park.

She had kept herself from hoping that Lord Powell would meet her there, for there was always the possibility, as Penelope had said, that he had simply amused himself with her company at Lady Winsome's for lack of anyone better to talk to. Lord Owens had told her that he was never seen with young ladies, and Susan could think of no reason why he should have found her an exception. Thus it was with a shock of genuine surprise that she saw him posting his horse, a handsome chestnut, toward her.

He doffed his hat in greeting, and Susan remarked to herself as to how very well the blue jacket and Hessian boots he was wearing suited him. As for herself, she supposed that she should be sorry that she was not dressed more in the latest style with a lawn gown and short jacket which opened wide at the front. But to Susan riding was a serious business, even when engaged in a tame London park, and she wore the same rather shabby habit which she wore when galloping across Somerset meadows with a sort of jockey cap which she had kept for ages because it suited her pulled over her curls.

"Miss Collins," he said.

"Lord Powell," she replied.

For a moment there was a certain restraint between them as their horses moved restlessly this way and that; and then he smiled.

"I suppose that I should say that this is a great surprise," he said, "but the truth of the matter is that I remembered your saying that you rode here most mornings and hoped to meet you."

Susan's cheeks felt hot, but she hoped she was

not flushing. She had liked Lord Powell very much on their first meeting and she did not want him to think that she felt any girlish flutterings at seeing him again. Remembering how open their conversation over supper at Lady Winsome's had been, she decided to be honest.

"I'm glad to see you, sir," she said evenly.

Again a moment of restraint passed over them.

"And may I ask if you and your sister were able to settle the matter of Sir Edwin," he said keeping his dark eyes on hers. "It was such a strange thing to have happen that I confess to curiosity. And then, of course, there was your distress. You hid it well enough, but the thought of it troubled me."

To her surprise, Susan felt no constraint about telling him what had passed between her and Penelope. As she talked, they began to canter together with the ease of accomplished horsemen.

"Well, at least you understand her motives," he said when she had finished. "And that is something. No doubt, as she said, it was a whim. But vicious, none the less. You must keep an eye on her, I think, until you come to know her better."

Susan assured him that she would, and the talk passed on to more casual matters. His sister was, it seemed, in the throes of her first romance, and he could only hope that she had chosen wisely.

"Young girls so often do not know their own minds," he said, "and, at the present, my mother is too ill to advise her."

At that Susan asked about Lady Powell and saw

his eyes grow hooded as he explained that her illness was primarily due to the stress of a London season. He had, he said, tried to convince his mother to return to their estate in Kent, but she would not hear of it.

"And yet the wholesome air would do her good, I'm sure," Susan declared. "Here in London we simply move from one crowded room to another. I cannot tell you how glad I am that we were able to take a house in Grosvenor Square so that I can easily get here to ride before breakfast."

"So you live in Grosvenor Square," Lord Powell said reflectively. "I have an engagement in your neighborhood this afternoon. A curious affair that. I received a note yesterday from an old friend of my grandfather's. I have never met the gentleman, but he seems most intent on seeing me at the earliest opportunity."

How easily they talked with one another, Susan thought, quite as though they had known one another forever.

"Lord Failfoot must be very old indeed," Lord Powell continued, "for he and my grandfather were at school together more than sixty years ago."

"Lord Failfoot, did you say?" Susan exclaimed.

"Why, yes," he said, glancing at her curiously. "Don't tell me that you know him. I have heard that he is a great recluse, which makes me wonder why he has come to the city when it is at its most crowded."

"Lord Failfoot is my great-uncle," Susan murmured, almost apologetically. "He came to us quite unexpectedly the day after Lady Winsome's ball."

She found that her heart was beating violently. Whatever her great-uncle was up to, she mistrusted it, and now to find that it involved this gentleman whom she found so congenial . . . She was certain that the old man could not know that they were acquainted, for she had said nothing of it nor had Lady Tangle and it was not the sort of thing her Aunt Lucinda would have seen fit to tell him, intent as she was in promoting Penelope's interests.

Lord Powell reared his horse to a halt. "How curious!" he said in a low voice. "And did he say nothing of having invited me?"

"He has never so much as mentioned your name," Susan said truthfully. "But then, he is such a strange old gentleman that one can never know what he will do next."

"Do you mean that he is senile?" Lord Powell asked her. "I only wish to be prepared."

"Oh, no. He has his wits about him," Susan said and went on to tell about the episode of the ear trumpet.

Lord Powell was duly amused. "He is a true eccentric then," he said. "I think I shall enjoy meeting him. But what do you think he wants of me? My grandfather once told me that the few times he tried to correspond with him after they left school, he met with rebuffs and insults. And yet, according to the letter I received, Lord Failfoot apparently considers my grandfather to have been his one true friend."

Even stranger, Susan thought, although she did not say it, was the fact that her granduncle had issued such an invitation all unbeknownst to her aunts, and she could not but wonder how Lady Hammerhead would respond to seeing Lord Powell arrive unexpected at her door.

But, as it happened, matters did not come to such a pass. When, after a gallop which left her cheeks rosy and her eyes sparkling, Susan had taken her leave of Lord Powell and returned to the house on Grosvenor Square, she found the others waiting impatiently for her in the breakfast room, the long windows of which looked out over a sunny rose garden. At her Aunt Lucinda's strict command, Susan joined them without first going upstairs to change, as was her habit.

"Your granduncle has something to say to us," Lady Tangle whispered as Susan took her place beside her at the round table. "He was quite dreadfully annoyed to find that you were not here when he came down to breakfast."

And then a silence fell as Lord Failfoot made a great business of clearing his throat. In the clear morning light he looked even more shrunken than usual. As was his custom, he was dressed in a voluminous dressing gown of ancient splendor and his periwig was tipped rakishly to one side of his head. It was clear that he had something of considerable importance to impart, his beady black eyes darting from face to face as he began to speak.

"There never was a contest worthy of the name without a prize," he said abruptly. "That's my consideration, at any rate, and you shall take it for what it is worth."

Lady Hammerhead and Penelope nodded in mute agreement, the latter keeping a stiff smile plastered to her lips, while Lady Tangle observed him with a degree of trepidation. As for Susan, she assumed a watchful air, determined not to be bullied.

"Now the money's one part of it," the old man went on. "One of the gels will get it all and good luck to you. But there's my decision, eh? Must have something to base it on. Even a fool could see that."

He passed his leer around the table as though it was a special dish. Lady Hammerhead and Penelope nodded their heads even more vehemently.

"Now, I've done a bit of inquiring," Lord Failfoot went on. "Had it done for me. Comes to the same thing. And I've decided that a certain eligible young gentleman will be the goal, in a manner of speaking. Going to turn you two gels loose on him, that's what. Grandfather a great friend of mine. Years ago. Never mind that. It all comes down to this. Whichever one of you gels can get him to offer himself is the one who gets my fortune. There now! Can't speak any clearer than that. Fellow'll be here this afternoon at four sharp. Expect to see you two waiting on the line."

"Oh, dear, oh, dear!" Lady Tangle murmured.

"What a perfectly extraordinary idea," Lady Hammerhead declared. "But very clever, of course. Very clever!"

"But what is his name, sir?" Penelope asked, her smile faltering. "Certainly we should know his name."

"Can't see that the name makes any difference," the old man grumbled. "But, if you must know, he's the Viscount Powell."

Sheer outrage blurred Susan's vision. She wanted to say that it was the most outrageous notion she had ever heard of. Not trusting herself to speak, she rose from the table and left the room.

# Chapter 7

"But it's not fair!" Penelope cried petulantly. "I told him that, but you know what he is. He quite refused to listen. Indeed he seemed to credit you with a certain wiliness, Susan. He said it was clever of you to have second-guessed him. But I think it goes deeper than that and Aunt Lucinda agrees. You must have known in advance that this was his plan!"

An hour had passed since Lord Failfoot's incredible announcement, and although Susan had tried, she had not been able to keep Lady Hammerhead and Penelope from joining her and her Aunt Dorothy in the latter's bedchamber.

Since she had been literally forced to speak to them, Susan determined to draw no quarter.

"Perhaps," she said crisply, "you will tell me precisely how I could have arranged to know about our granduncle's absurd idea."

"It must have been you, Dorothy!" Lady Hammerhead exclaimed, rounding on the frowsy little woman sitting in the corner, playing nervously with the ribbons of her mobcap.

"Yes!" Lady Hammerhead exclaimed, advancing in a threatening manner. "You have been more clever than I thought, all along. I thought to have a tie with the housekeeper was enough, but now I see that you must have had some closer recourse to him. Brattle, perhaps. No doubt a gentleman's valet knows all his secrets. And you learned this one in time to advise Susan to strike up a conversation with Lord Powell, to give her an edge!"

As she spoke, Lady Hammerhead shook her finger closer and closer to the tip of Lady Tangle's nose, with the result that, when she had said her last word, Lady Tangle looked as terrified as if she were about to be put upon. As for Reginald, he had been heaving restlessly beside Susan's chair and, when she deliberately released his collar, he sprang forward quite ferociously enough to cause Lady Hammerhead to break off her physical advance.

"I—I assure you that your suspicions are quite unjustified!" Lady Tangle told her. "Why, 'pon my word, I never thought . . ."

"Oh, it is all very well to protest," Penelope said in a shrill voice, "but you cannot ask us to believe, surely, that it was simply coincidence which led Susan to luring the very gentleman our granduncle has set up as goal to take her to supper not three nights ago."

Bent on following the trail of hostility against his mistress wherever it might lead, Reginald, hair stiff and teeth bared, took this opportunity to approach Penelope. Lulu, who had wrapped herself like a muff around Penelope's arm, began to bark hysterically.

"We are no better than our pets," Susan announced when both animals had been soothed and sent off in the care of the footman. "Squabbling over nothing. It was unkind of you, Aunt Lucinda, to think that Aunt Dorothy could have sunk to the sort of spying you accuse her of. Why, you must know by now that she is incapable of that sort of duplicity, however easily it may come to you and my sister."

She had not meant to say so much and saw, at once, that she had gone too far. Penelope uttered a little squeal of outrage, and Lady Hammerhead pressed both hands to her green satin turban as though she were afraid that it would fly straight off her head.

"You dare to accuse me of duplicity, my gel!" Lady Hammerhead shrilled. "Dorothy, you should be ashamed. Ashamed, I say! What sort of possible upbringing could produce this sort of rudeness!"

Lady Tangle quailed under the force of this fresh attack, and Susan saw tears rise in her eyes.

"There is no need for you to blame Aunt Dorothy," Susan said, going to put her arm about

81

Lady Tangle's neck. "No one could have had a happier girlhood than I, and all on her account. I will not have a word spoken against her guardianship of me, and neither will I stand by silent and hear her accused of scheming in the manner you suggest. She is far too fine a person for that. As for saying what I did to you, I am sorry for it. I lost my temper. And, I will remind you, that I am not the only one to have done so in the past few minutes."

"Well, well," Lady Hammerhead said more mildly. "No doubt we are wrong to set to quarreling in this way. But when I think that you had first chance at the prize . . ."

"I do not think that Lord Powell would like to hear of himself described in precisely that manner," Susan said dryly. "Somehow it strikes the wrong chord."

"But surely Granduncle has told him of his plan," Penelope said.

"On the contrary, clearly he has not," Susan told her. "I do not know the gentleman well, I admit, but well enough to know that if he knew what was in the wind, he would never have agreed to come here today."

What a flare she could throw in the fire, she thought, if she were to add that, having ridden with him this morning, she knew for a fact that he was as innocent of Lord Failfoot's scheme as all of them had been an hour before.

"There is another thing," Susan went on. "I have not changed my mind about my conduct in the matter. When our granduncle proposed to make one of us heiress on certain terms which he did not clearly define, except that competition of a sort was expected, I said that I would have no part of it. My decision has only been reinforced by his plan to implicate Lord Powell. As a consequence, I have spent the time since breakfast discussing with my aunt the desirability of our returning to the country at once."

The news clearly pleased Penelope. Indeed, she darted across the room to kiss her sister in a rare show of affection.

"No doubt that is a wise decision, my dear," Lady Hammerhead said benevolently. "You have made no secret of the fact that the *haut ton's* doings do not interest you. Why, indeed, prolong the boredom. Penelope and I would do very well here by ourselves. You need not fear that your leaving would inconvenience us, particularly since the rest of this house has been paid for the season."

"However," she resumed, "Aunt Dorothy seems to think that Mama would have wanted me to spend an entire season in London. She assures me that a simple coming-out is not enough and that, were she to agree to my idea to return to Tangle Hall, she would have somehow failed in her responsibility."

Penelope drew away at once and Lady Hammerhead's face fell.

"But then, of course," she said, "your Mama can scarcely know . . ."

"That does not matter!" Lady Tangle exclaimed with unusual vehemence, bouncing up and down in her chair in her excitement. "Dear Kate often spoke of her hopes for both her daughters, and I could never face myself if I did not give Susan the opportunity to—to . . ."

"To marry well?" Susan said in a low voice. "You know the prospect holds no great appeal for me, aunt."

"Well, if it does not, then it should!" Lady Tangle said with a firmness she did not often muster. "At least you must give yourself a chance to meet someone who might be agreeable. I would not rest quiet in my grave if I should think that I had had a part in depriving you of the—the proper opportunities."

"Ah, well," Susan said in a low voice. "We have had this discussion before. Pray do not speak of graves, Aunt Dorothy. I have always obeyed you in important matters and I see that this is one of such to you. And so, I will remain in London. But I will take no part in such an absurb hunt as our granduncle has suggested. He seems to see Penelope and me as two hounds set in chase of a stag."

"You must guard yourself against picking up your Aunt Dorothy's fondness for the unusual metaphor," Lady Hammerhead warned her. "But this is by-the-by. What do you intend to do this afternoon when Lord Powell comes to visit, pray? Remain in your room?"

"I should like to do nothing better," Susan said and paused. She had already given the matter of Lord Powell's visit some consideration. Had she not been told by him himself that he was coming, she would not have hesitated to have made some excuse and remained secluded. But, as matters stood, she knew that he would be fairly puzzled were she not to appear, and think, perhaps, that she sought to avoid him. Somehow the idea of that gave her pain. After all, he knew nothing of Lord Failfoot's plan, and as a consequence, it would scarcely be fair to punish him with the casual insult of not appearing. It came to her that she owed it to him to inform him of the old man's absurd notion. He must know, in advance, that he was being used. How better could she thank him for having saved her from Sir Edwin Gingerton's attack?

But that would come later. This afternoon she would be pleasant but reserved. They were certain to meet again, if not in the park then elsewhere. And then she would find an opportunity to tell him what he must know.

She became aware that Lady Hammerhead and Penelope, with breath quite literally bated, were waiting for her to continue.

"However, in simple politeness to Granduncle, I will join his guest," she went on.

"Oh, how sly you are!" Penelope exclaimed. "You pretend to want to retire to the country, but do not for such fine reasons! You wish to remain in your room this afternoon, but will not for fear of seeming to be impolite!"

"I will not interfere with your flirtation, if that is what you really mean," Susan said in a low voice.

"Sly and coy to boot!" Penelope retorted, flouncing out of the room.

"Indeed, I think you are cleverer than I had thought," Lady Hammerhead said thoughtfully before she followed her niece. "But we will see what we will see, my dear. The cleverness is not all on your side, you know."

When they had left, Susan threw herself on the chaise longue by the window in a perfect fit of temper.

"Oh, how I wish I did not find so much to dislike in them!" she cried. "How I wish that we had never come to London! How I wish that Granduncle had a proper heir, in which case none of this would ever have had to happen!"

Lady Tangle released the ribbons of her mobcap.

"But, my dear!" she exclaimed. "Of course he has an heir. I thought that I had told you that long ago."

Whereupon, in her customary way, she promptly changed the subject and began to speculate on which gown she should wear for Lord Powell's visit.

"La, my dear," she told Susan. "If, when I saw you supping with him the other evening at Lady Winsome's, I had ever thought . . ."

"But Aunt Dorothy!" Susan cried. "You must go on about Lord Failfoot's heir. What you have said makes no sense at all. If he has someone to inherit his title, then why should he be thinking of leaving Susan and me his fortune?"

Lady Tangle rose and bounced across the floor to look out the window in the mode of one keenly interested in the weather. But Susan was not to be put off so easily.

"Tell me, Aunt," she insisted. "Given the circumstances, surely I have a right to know everything."

"Such an unpleasantness," Lady Tangle murmured. "And it happened so long ago, well over thirty years. It ought by rights to be forgotten."

"I am not interested in whatever happened as gossip," Susan persisted, taking her aunt by the arm. "I know you have a great distaste for *that*. But, at the moment, I feel I must know."

"Ah, well," Lady Tangle sighed. "I can tell what I know of it quickly enough. His lordship quarreled with his son. James, his name was, and they both had quick tempers. I do not know what it was all about, although no doubt Lucinda can tell you if you ask, since she makes it a point to know details and such. But the fact of the matter is that James was sent packing. Disinherited. The Failfoot estate is not entailed, you see, more's the pity."

"But Lord Failfoot must pass on his title to his son," Susan said quickly. "Oh, if only they could be

87

reconciled—and surely after so many years it might be possible—all of this business could be forgotten."

"Well, as for that," Lady Tangle said uneasily, "James died not ten years after he'd been sent away. Old Lady Failfoot was quite brokenhearted by it all. In fact it was she who told me about it. A notice came from a solicitor saying that James was dead and that, in his last illness, he had ordered that not more than that should be told. His life was to be a blank to his father from the moment of his leaving the house."

"But there might have been a wife and children!" Susan exclaimed. "Surely enquiries were made!"

"That was what Lady Failfoot wanted," her aunt told her. "But she went to her own deathbed not knowing any more than that her son was gone forever. It is a sad story and, 'pon my soul, I do not like to think about it."

As for Susan, she could do no more than agree that it made a sorry tale. For the first time she found herself pitying her granduncle. Hard-nosed and stubborn as he was, he had condemned himself to an old age of loneliness and, no doubt, regret. What a pretty end it had all come to when he could think of nothing better to do with his fortune than to attempt to lure two girls he scarcely knew to marry the grandson of a friend he had not seen since school days! His narrow mind had nothing to fasten on except the infallibility of greed. She could only hope that once he had met Lord Powell, he would see that his play was an impossible one.

In the event that he did not, however, Susan promised herself that she would tell Lord Powell the truth.

# Chapter 8

But, as it happened, Lord Failfoot was far from discouraged from his scheme after meeting Lord Powell. Susan had hoped that the old man would see that here was a gentleman who should not be involved, even indirectly, and unwittingly, in such a scheme as he had in mind, but although her granduncle had no difficulty at all in seeing Lord Powell's sterling qualities, his own twisted sense of right and wrong did not permit him to understand that his old friend's grandson should not be used as a pawn.

"Damned decent chap, that," he declared when the visit had ended. "And you made a set for him right enough, gel," he added, leering at Penelope.

And, indeed, Penelope had unleashed all her charms for the occasion. To begin with, she had made no attempt to accentuate her similarity to her twin but had appeared in one of her Parisian gowns, a pale blue affair of silk with bodice cut so low as to make Lady Tangle gasp and Susan wonder. Under Lady Hammerhead's approving eye, Penelope had been at her most graceful best, chatting inconsequentially of France and, after finding that Lord Powell more frequently visited Italy, lapsing into that native tongue with ease and speaking at length, Susan guessed, of the delights of Florence and Rome.

Still, her sister had been clever enough not to push herself too far. She had encouraged Lord Powell to reminisce about his grandfather with the result that Lord Failfoot and the young man were soon at ease with one another. There were schoolboy tales to be told, and his lordship told them well enough to amuse even Susan, who remained at a distance, smiling pleasantly when Lord Powell glanced in her direction, but not engaging in the general conversation except when necessary. Indeed, she could feel her face burn whenever she thought of the absolute necessity of telling him, at some future time, the real reason why he had been invited to the house in Grosvenor Square.

Down the hall Susan could hear her sister laughing, and she knew, too well, the cause of her excitement. In Penelope's opinion, at least, she had dazzled Lord Powell. Add to that the fact that Lady Hammerhead had managed to determine, before he had left them, that he was to accompany his sister to the same soirée at Lady Cartley's which they were to attend that evening.

Pausing in her own toilette, Susan remembered the rather puzzled glance Lord Powell had shot at her as he was leaving. No doubt it was a mystery to him why she had preferred to stay so much in the background during his visit, scarcely uttering a word. He was, she thought, certain to make a point of speaking to her this evening, and then she must tell him everything.

Propping her elbows on the dressing table, she cupped her face in her hands and stared at herself intently in the mirror. It would be an embarrassment for her to speak to him honestly, since, after all, Lord Failfoot *was* her relative. There was also the nagging sense of being someone who told tales out of school. After all, he was a grown man and a sophisticate to boot. Surely he did not need her protection. No, the reason that she felt impelled to tell him of her granduncle's scheme was that, unless she did, she could no longer indulge herself in the pleasure of his company. For, if she did, and he were later to find out, he would, of necessity, believe that she had been motivated by her granduncle to make a play for him.

Oh, it was so complicated, Susan fretted. It took away the pleasure she might have enjoyed at the thought of meeting him again. Had he not so clearly liked Lord Failfoot, it might have been easier to make such a disclosure.

So troubled was she that Susan said very little in

the carriage on the way to the entertainment, and Penelope, taking her silence as pique that she had had the center of attention that afternoon, took pleasure in taunting her.

"I expect that you thought that Lord Powell would find you enigmatic this afternoon," she whispered as they rattled along the cobbled street. "But I do not think, sister, that the role of the mysterious lady suits you well. With gentlemen of the world it is always better to shine and sparkle, I assure you."

Susan did not take the trouble to answer, and when they entered the ballroom, which was already hot and crowded, she took the first opportunity to separate herself and her Aunt Dorothy from her sister and her guardian. But Penelope seemed destined to claim her attention, for no sooner had she settled Lady Tangle in a quiet corner than she saw her "other aunt" marching up to Lord Powell, who was standing on the other side of the room, with Penelope gliding languidly in her wake. There was a brief conversation with most of the talking being done by Lady Hammerhead, and then Susan saw her sister take Lord Powell's arm and advance onto the dance floor where a cotillion line was being formed.

Forcing herself to be objective, Susan had to admit that Penelope was the essence of grace and chic. Since it was clearly not to her advantage to dress like her twin sister this evening, she was wearing an empire style evening dress of a light amber velvet with a deeply cut oval neckline and highly puffed short sleeves, while her long, white gloves drew attention to her slender arms. She had even done her hair differently tonight, skillfully smoothing out the curls and pulling it into a chignon into which she had woven a string of tiny, velvet flowers. As Penelope laughed and chatted with Lord Powell while they stood waiting for the music to start, it came to Susan that he might, indeed, be intrigued by her. After all, he had traveled extensively on the Continent and, no doubt, had come to appreciate the airs which Penelope had been at such pains to cultivate in Paris. Granted that he knew of the trick Penelope had attempted with Sir Edwin Gingerton, but, for all she knew, he might be quite willing to overlook it in the name of playfulness.

She could see Lord Owens wandering about the outskirts of the crowd, looking right and left, and thought it more than possible that he was searching for her. But, being in no mood to dance, she remained beside her aunt where it was possible, when his eyes turned in her direction, to move in such a way as to prevent him from seeing her.

It was clear from the anxious way that Lady Tangle looked at her that she knew something was wrong. As the music lilted and the dancers whirled up and down the floor, Susan thought that she had never felt so awkward and alone.

But, of course, she could not remain unobserved for long. A gentleman with whom she was faintly acquainted claimed her for the next dance, and directly it had ended, she found herself looking up into Lord Powell's dark eyes.

"If you will allow me, sir," he said, bowing to her companion, "I would like to invite Miss Collins to walk with me on the terrace."

Now that the time had come, Susan took a deep breath. No doubt when she had told him, Lord Powell would scorn her entire family, herself included. No matter. She could not help it if he did. Anything was better than allowing him to think that she had, even for a moment, taken part in such a scheme.

Lady Cartley's ballroom, unlike Lady Winsome's, was located on the ground floor, and because of the heat, the long windows opening onto a terrace had been opened. Great stone urns had been planted with sweet-smelling flowers, and the moon was high overhead. Troubled as she was, however, Susan could not see the romance of the moment as she strolled along with one hand lightly on Lord Powell's arm.

She had meant to speak at once, but before she had a chance to do so, he paused and turned to her.

"I wanted the opportunity to tell you that I think your granduncle is an extraordinarily fine old gentleman," he said. "Whatever has caused him to cease being a recluse I do not know, but he is nothing like what my grandfather led me to expect. The eccentricity is there, of course. One can see it in his manner. But it is clear he has mellowed since the days when he sent his only son packing."

"You know of that?" Susan exclaimed.

"Yes," Lord Powell assured her. "And it is because I know not only that but other things as well that I am taking the liberty of confiding in you. You see, having met the old man, I think that there are certain steps I must take. But I must have your opinion first."

The urgency with which he spoke drove all other thoughts from Susan's mind.

"It is no liberty," she assured him. "Anything that concerns my granduncle concerns me, as well."

"Well, it is this then," he went on quickly, drawing her into the shadows as another couple came walking by. "You know, of course, that Lord Failfoot's son died not many years after being exiled from his father's estate."

Susan only nodded, not wanting to interrupt him with an explanation that she had only learned of it this afternoon.

"My grandfather told me what I will tell you next in the greatest confidence," Lord Powell said in a low voice. "The information must still be treated as a secret, you understand. James, the son, told my grandfather everything shortly before his death. In confidence. But, because it was so important, my grandfather made me his confidant, in turn, during his last illness. He said he thought it only right that someone should know that James had married and had a son."

"A son!" Susan exclaimed.

"We must speak quietly," Lord Powell warned her. "It seems that Lord Failfoot's son so despised his father that he changed his name and married under it. Even his wife did not know the truth of his background, that he was heir to a title, if nothing else."

"You mean that when my granduncle dies, there is somewhere a young man who does not know that he is an Earl!" Susan whispered.

"That is precisely what I *do* mean," Lord Powell told her. "And that young man is not 'somewhere.' He is here in London. His name is also James. James Rhodes. He is a barrister of some promise. A perfect gentleman and my friend."

Susan could scarcely take in the news, coming all at once as it had. And yet she knew, somehow, that Lord Powell depended on her to be calm and sensible

"You know him and yet you have never told him all this?" she said.

"Perhaps it was wrong of me," Lord Powell admitted. "But it was his father's dying wish that he know nothing of his heritage. And I had heard such tales of Lord Failfoot's irascibility and ill temper that I thought that nothing good could come from saying anything which might, quite possibly, cause James to seek a meeting with the old man. It seemed only logical that history would repeat itself and that there would be an ugly scene. And yet now, having met your granduncle and finding him quite unlike his reputation, I have had second thoughts."

Susan's mind worked quickly. Clearly she could no longer think of telling him about Lord Failfoot's scheme, since this would cause Lord Powell's good opinion of the old man to go flying. She was fortunate that he had confided all of this in her before she had a chance to speak. Clearly it was to everyone's advantage to reconcile the grandson with his unknown grandfather. And yet she knew, better than Lord Powell, how small a chance there was that her granduncle would be as mellow as he had pretended to be this afternoon when confronted by his rightful heir.

"I can see that this must have troubled you greatly," she said slowly. "There are the wishes of the father to consider."

"It does not seem right, however, that, because of an ancient quarrel, a young man should never know who he really is," Lord Powell said. "I will confess to you that I had already decided that, once your granduncle had died, I would let James know the truth. Allow him to weigh his father's desires in the matter against his own. Make it possible for him to claim the title if he wished, or keep his past identity."

"It will come as a great shock to him," Susan said softly. "You said you wanted my advice, sir. I think that it would be unwise to introduce my granduncle's grandson to him. Granted that you saw the gentle side of Lord Failfoot's nature this afternoon, but I have reason to think that there is still a hard core of his old self remaining."

"And yet," Lord Powell murmured, "there is the chance they might be reconciled. If I wait to tell James until after his grandfather's death, there will be nothing but the title for him, if he wishes it. If, somehow, the two could be brought together before that time, the estate and title might be kept together, as they should."

Once again Susan was glad that she had had no chance to tell him what Lord Failfoot's present plans were for the inheritance of his fortune. The scheme seemed even sadder and shabbier now that she knew he had a rightful heir. In an instant she determined that she would do whatever she could to help the unknown James Rhodes to gain his proper heritage.

"What do you think of this idea?" she said slowly, trying to formulate the notion which had just come into her head. "You say that Mr. Rhodes is your friend and a gentleman."

"No one could be more agreeable," Lord Powell assured her. "He is intelligent and sensitive. There is no one I know I can speak of more highly."

"If that is the case," Susan went on, "might it not be an excellent idea if my granduncle could come to know him *as* James Rhodes? *As* your friend, and nothing more? Is it not just possible that the two might take to one another. If Mr. Rhodes were to gain my granduncle's respect—indeed, perhaps his affection——there might come the moment when it would be safe to reveal all."

Lord Powell took her gloved hand in his and pressed it.

"An excellent idea, Miss Collins!" he exclaimed. "I was certain that I could depend on you! As far as James is concerned, he will only be being taken to meet an interesting old friend of my grandfather's. Lord Failfoot pressed me to visit him again, if you recall."

Susan was glad of the shadows, for, had there been light, some chance expression on her face might have hinted at her sense of the irony of what he had just said. Now he must never know just why her granduncle had been so eager to have him return to the house in Grosvenor Square.

"There is one thing," Lord Powell went on. "I would like to have you meet James first. You know your granduncle far better than I, and if you met James, you would be able to make a better guess than I as to whether he and Lord Failfoot will strike it off."

"Yes, there is that," Susan murmured. "Besides, I would like very much to meet your friend."

"Your cousin," Lord Powell reminded her.

Susan laughed. The shock which she had first felt on hearing this news was wearing off, and she was aware of a great sense of relief that, with any luck, the business of her granduncle's fortune would no longer be a burden to her.

"How odd it is," she said, "to have such a close

101

relative whom I have never met. Yes. I will meet him if it can be quietly arranged."

"The park, I think," Lord Powell said in a low voice.

"The park on Sunday morning," Susan agreed. "There will be nothing odd in my taking my usual ride alone."

"James will know nothing," Lord Powell told her. "He and I will ride together and happen to meet a young lady of my acquaintance. Nothing could be easier."

"And yet we must be very careful," Susan murmured, very much aware now that he had not yet released her hand.

"We will be conspirators together," Lord Powell assured her. "And, I must tell you, Miss Collins, that there is no one I would trust more."

# Chapter 9

By unspoken agreement, they did not meet again that evening. Instinctively Susan felt that it was best, if they were to conspire to introduce James Rhodes to the house on Grosvenor Square, that they should not be seen together, and apparently, Lord Powell felt the same. As a result, the remainder of the evening seemed to drag itself through Susan's fingers, although she danced every dance and went to supper with the familiar Lord Owens whose chatter was of such a superficial, albeit pleasant, nature that she was free to let her mind wander where it would. And, at the end of whatever path she chose, Lord Powell always was waiting. He was so vividly set in her mind that Susan allowed herself the idle fancy that he was more real there than was the dark, lean man with the searching eyes who sat with his sister and her beau at the further end of the table.

Susan was happier than she had ever expected to be. It was a strange feeling, a curious excitement combined with a tremulous sensation. She could not describe it, even to herself, but she knew the cause. Lord Powell had trusted and admired her enough to choose to confide in her without preamble or hesitation. He had assumed that she would advise him well, and it seemed, she had not disappointed him. And what a fine secret it was they shared! If they were careful, if they moved slowly and cautiously, it might be that a young man would receive his full inheritance complete. Better even than that was the possibility that old wounds might be healed, for although her granduncle's scheme had appalled Susan, she wanted nothing but happiness for him. Indeed, she was in a forgiving mood even in regard to his plan for her and Penelope, for although the original fault might well have been primarily his, it must have hurt him to know that his son had died unreconciled, a stranger with another name. To have lived with such agony for half a century was enough to have twisted even the finest mind.

But there were steps to consider, and Susan indulged herself in examining them even while she was listening, with one part of her mind, to Lord Owens talk. First she must meet James Rhodes and determine whether or not she thought that Lord Failfoot would take to him as he had taken to Lord

Powell. The young man would not come to him with Lord Powell's recommendations, of course. She would do well to remember that. Mr. Rhodes would appear simply as a young barrister with no fortune or title to recommend him. He would not have the advantage of being a relative of one of the old man's friends: Certainly he could not be counted as an eligible suitor. He would succeed or fail on the strength of his own character, and Susan did not know her granduncle well enough as yet to be certain what character alone would mean to him.

Might it be possible that some chord might be struck between the two, without either knowing of their true relationship, she wondered? She believed in the power of intuition and it might be that old man and young would sense a sudden bond. And, as she thought of that, it occurred to her that it was possible that James Rhodes might bear so much resemblance to his father that all would be given away. The idea gave her a moment's pause, and she wished that it was possible that she might signal Lord Powell with her eyes so that he would come to her and she might ask him if he had ever seen Lord Failfoot's son, if there was indeed a resemblance.

But there was nothing she could do except determine that she would find a way to ask him tomorrow in the park, if it was possible for her to do it then out of Mr. Rhodes's hearing. She became aware that people were rising from the table, that the soirée was coming to an end. She looked up to see that Lord Powell, with his sister on his arm, was leaving the room. But he had paused by the door, and she knew, as their eyes met, that he had waited to say a silent goodbye.

Later, in the lozenged coach, Lady Hammerhead showed herself to be in the best of good spirits. Nothing would do but that Penelope should tell them every detail of what Lord Powell had said to her.

"How disappointed you must be, my dear," Lady Hammerhead said to Susan, "that he did not ask you to take the floor with him this evening. But then, since you made so little effort to entertain him when he visited us this afternoon, you would have been foolish to expect that he would.

"I hope you were not *too* disappointed, love," Lady Tangle whispered, and in the darkness, Susan smiled and squeezed her aunt's hand reassuringly, thinking of the chaos she would create if she were to tell them all that she had walked for a half hour at least with the gentleman in question on the terrace and shared an intimate discussion with him.

But revelations of that sort must come later, she knew, if at all. It was of the utmost importance that neither her Aunt Lucinda nor her sister guess that she and Lord Powell shared a secret and a common aim. Neither must they guess the true identity of Mr. Rhodes when they met him, for if they did, Susan knew that both would do everything in their power to keep Lord Failfoot from being reconciled with his grandson. Given the circumstances, she could not even tell her Aunt Dorothy the truth. Lord Failfoot must be the first to know and then only if it seemed that he might be willing to forget the past.

The old man was waiting up for them at the house on Grosvenor Square despite the lateness of the hour. With his gouty leg propped high on cushions and a bottle of brandy at hand, he had questioned both girls closely about the evening's activities and, having heard the details of Penelope's little coup, had the gall to remind Susan that she must make a better effort or it would be no contest. At that, Lady Tangle had glanced anxiously at her ward, no doubt fearing an explosion of temper or, at the very least, a denial that she was running any race. But Susan had contented herself with bidding her granduncle a quiet good-night and leaving him to the kind offices of her sister and Lady Hammerhead.

Sunday morning Susan was early to arrive at the park. Once the groom had helped her to mount, she dismissed him with a smile, murmuring that for this once there was no need for him to return in an hour.

"There is so little traffic on the street that I can easily ride back to the square alone," she told him.

Alfred was an old man who was the only retainer she and her aunt had brought down from the country, and she knew him well enough to note the speculative expression in his faded blue eyes and guessed that he had thought at once of an assignation. Still, she could trust him to say nothing, she knew, and she rode on into the park toward the spot where she and Lord Powell had encountered one another before, aware of a pleasant quickening of anticipation.

It was very peaceful at this time in the morning, with no one in sight and the trees throwing their branches to the breeze. Bird song and the flowers which dotted the grass reminded Susan of the country. She had been happier there, she thought, but certainly there had never been any excitement to challenge her. Would she miss London, she wondered. It was a question she had never asked herself before because always, in the past, the answer had been so quick to come to her. But now something had changed. She had, she knew, no more use for the ways of the *haut ton* than she had had before, and yet . . .

So lost in thought was she that the two riders had nearly reached her before she looked up. Lord Powell sat easily on his chestnut bay, but the gentleman who cantered beside him on a dappled gray seemed to sit uneasily in the saddle, as though riding was not his forte. He was, however, dressed as correctly as his companion in topboots and breeches and, as he came abreast of her, Susan noted his pleasant good looks which reflected nothing of Lord Failfoot's sharp-boned features.

Both gentlemen doffed their hats in greeting, and Lord Powell murmured an introduction. She was glad to see that he did not make an elaborate pretense of not having expected to see her. Neither was there any hint that they had arranged to meet. It was a casual encounter, nothing more, and for a moment he spoke about the soirée of the evening before in just such a fashion as to insure that Mr. Rhodes would know that their acquaintance was on an ordinary footing.

"Miss Collins comes from Somerset," Lord Powell said by way of including his friend in the conversation.

"Do you indeed?" Mr. Rhodes replied. "I have friends there. Perhaps you know Squire Headington then? His son and I studied for the bar together."

Susan confessed that she did indeed know the squire, and his son, as well, all the time thinking of how clever Lord Powell had been to have thought of this device of providing her and Mr. Rhodes with something in common. No doubt if mention of Somerset had not provided a topic of conversation, he had been prepared with other possibilities. Certainly there was a confidence about him which indicated that he had not arranged this encounter without making preparation for it. She blamed herself for not having had the forethought to have realized that since she and Mr. Rhodes presumably moved in different social circles in London, a common interest might have been difficult to come upon on the spur of the moment.

But, as it was, everything went easily enough. Riding between her and Lord Powell, the young barrister discoursed amusingly on the difficulties

Squire Headington had had in arranging the marriages of seven daughters and his son's doleful predictions that he would be left with an abundance of spinster sisters to care for.

"Ah, but that has been taken care of at last," Susan said. "You must have heard the three youngest accomplished the impossible in unison, so to speak. All three are to marry farmers whose land adjoins that of their father. My aunt and I received a letter to that effect only last week from Frances, who is the eldest, as you know. There is, I take it, a general air of rejoicing at Headington Hall, and she said that now, at last, she had great hopes for herself, since the Fates seemed to be smiling."

James Rhodes laughed at that and declared himself well pleased, even though he could not be as sanguine as the eldest Miss Headington appeared to be, given her temper which was so volatile as to have provided her with a certain reputation which frightened suitors off. One thing led to another so easily that Susan was surprised to find that they had come to the end of the bridle path. While Mr. Rhodes was turning his horse, she flashed a smile at Lord Powell to let him know the extent of her approval of his friend.

"Then you think we may proceed?" he murmured to her as they parted, Mr. Rhodes being distracted by his mount's sudden decision to break into a more spirited gait.

It was the moment for Susan to ask if there were

any strong resemblance between Mr. Rhodes and his father, and Lord Powell shook his head.

"To my knowledge, I never met the gentleman," he said, "and so I cannot tell. But I think that is a chance we must take."

"You will bring him with you when you call next then?" she said.

"And that as soon as possible," Lord Powell replied. "The sooner this matter is resolved the better, I think. Will your aunts be receiving company tomorrow afternoon, do you know?"

"If you were to drop Lady Hammerhead a note stating your intention to make a visit, you will be assured of a warm welcome," Susan told him dryly.

Just how warm Penelope and her "other aunt" would welcome him, had they the chance, she hoped he would never know.

# Chapter 10

"How delightful it is that Lord Powell intends to make us another visit so soon!" Penelope announced the next morning when Susan came into the breakfast room to find her twin alone. "But then, perhaps you had not heard. Aunt Lucinda has just told Aunt Dorothy, and they have just now gone up to tell the old gaffer, who is certain to be well pleased."

Susan thought, not for the first time, that it was odd that her sister, who always made such a fuss about their granduncle in his presence, should refer to him so informally in his absence, but she made no comment. Instead she helped herself to bread and butter and poured a cup of tea, waiting for the monologue she knew must follow.

It was clear that Penelope had decided that Lord Powell's return visit was because of her, for there was a smug expression on her sister's face as she nibbled at one of the croissants which Lady Hammerhead insisted that cook bake each morning to accompany the thick hot chocolate which she assured everyone was the only civilized sort of breakfast.

"Aunt Lucinda received a note by the early post," Penelope continued in her self-satisfied manner. "It has a certain significance, I think, that he should address himself to her rather than to Aunt Dorothy."

Susan agreed that it must, not seeing fit to reveal that she had received a message from the same source, albeit with no crested seal, Lord Powell having desired to remind her that they must make no secret of their "accidental" meeting in the park.

"It came to me afterward that it would seem odd to James if I asked him to pretend he had not met you before when we make our visit this afternoon," he had written. "Perhaps this has occurred to you, as well. No doubt you will want to mention the encounter to your aunts and sisters this morning or perhaps you have already spoken of it. You will excuse me for prompting you, but I know that you care as much about the success of our project as I."

He had signed himself simply Oliver, and Susan had spent some time staring at the name. What a strange and formal society it was in which someone she felt she knew as well as he should have had to disclose his Christian name in such a manner. The implication was not lost on her, and it had hurt her to have to crumple the note and burn it, although she knew how essential it was that no one in this household know that she had heard from him.

"Lord Powell has asked leave to bring a friend," Penelope continued, obviously delighted to be the source of so much information. "A Mr. Rhodes, I believe. I have been puzzling over that and I think it must be that he kindly thinks to offer you some distraction while he talks with me. Indeed, I think that it must mean that he plans a tête-à-tête between us. It is so difficult to talk intimately at soirées such as the one we attended the other evening, of course. When we danced I had the impression that he would have preferred a quiet chat, and now, you see, he has made plans to have one. Indeed, I will take pains to see that he does not allow our granduncle to bore him overlong."

It was wonderful, Susan thought, how her sister had misinterpreted. Still, she supposed it was logical enough for everyone to see any given situation to their own advantage. Still, it made it easier for her to confide that she had already met Mr. Rhodes and found him a very pleasant gentleman indeed.

"Lord Powell was riding with him, you say?" Penelope demanded, instantly alert. "How strange you did not see fit to mention it on your return from the park, Sister."

Susan searched her mind for a logical excuse and was relieved to remember that, when she had entered the house the morning before, Lulu and Reginald had been engaged in a battle in the front hall and that it had taken the united efforts of the household to pull them apart.

"What a strange person you are," Penelope said when Susan had completed her explanation. "I declare that it would have taken more than a dog fight to make me forget such an encounter. Pray, did Lord Powell ask after me?"

"He expressed a desire to visit again," Susan hedged, not wishing to lie outright. "It was clear that he was very eager to come. We did not speak long."

"How I wish I had been with you!" Penelope exclaimed. "I warrant the conversation would have been more extended if I had been there. Still, I am glad that it happened as it did, for, no doubt, it gave him the idea of bringing Mr. Rhodes with him to amuse you."

Delighted that her sister had so readily evolved a rationale for James Rhodes's visit, Susan readied herself for the young man's first encounter with his grandfather with an easy mind. Lord Failfoot would be in a good humor, thinking only to witness the next step in Penelope's or her own "capture" of Lord Powell and would, no doubt, be in a mood to welcome the young viscount's friend. Add to that the fact that Mr. Rhodes was clearly intelligent and vastly good-natured and there was, she thought, the possibility of a happy ending. As to how many encounters should take place between the old man and his grandson before either or both of them was told the truth, that was a matter which she and Lord Powell must decide.

However, when she descended to the drawing room at a little before three that afternoon, Susan was reminded of the lines of one of her favorite modern poets, Robert Burns, for it did indeed seem that the best laid plans of mice and men often did go astray. Far from finding her granduncle in a mellow mood, she discovered that, his gout having given him the greatest discomfort all day long, he was in an evil temper with the result that he had set both the aunts and Penelope, not to mention Reginald and Lulu, at bay with his cane, which he was wielding wildly to the accompaniment of violent oaths, many of which Susan had not heard before.

"Damme, woman!" Lord Failfoot declared, pointing his cane at Lady Hammerhead who glared back at him defiantly. "When I want medical advice I'll call a doctor!"

"I only thought you ought to know that if you set out to drink a bottle of claret, sir, you risk aggravating the attack," Lady Hammerhead said in a nasal voice. "Surely you realize that I only have your comfort in mind."

"Tittle-tattle!" Lord Failfoot shouted. "What you mean, madam, is that you would just as well have me stay alive until I've made a new will!"

Lady Hammerhead reared herself up stiffly to her full height, which, due to the rather high, green satin turban she was wearing, was considerable.

"You are quite wrong if you think that, sir!

117

Nothing could be further from my mind than your will."

"Ha! I suppose you were not thinking of my fortune when you decked that niece of yours up like a common jade, madam! Answer me that, eh! No holds barred, eh! She's to win the prize willy-nilly, what?"

Glancing at her sister, Susan realized what he meant. Penelope had chosen to array herself in one of her Parisian gowns, this one an elegant but daring affair of pale blue silk which clung to her body so closely that the lines of her slender hips and legs were clearly visible. The broad velvet band which was tied just below the breasts had been drawn so tight that they seemed to swell from the confines of the bodice, which was cut even lower than that of the gown she had worn for Lord Powell's last visit. Since the recent revolution had made jewelry unpopular with French ladies of fashion, Penelope wore none, but she had, Susan noted, attached a beauty spot close to the base of her creamy white throat, and her golden hair was caught with a fillet of silk bows which matched her gown.

"I assure you that my niece is dressed in the finest Continental mode, sir!" Lady Hammerhead was saying in an outraged voice. "Being an experienced traveler, Lord Powell is certain to appreciate the latest style. Simple because gels like Susan choose to dress like milkmaids is no reason that my niece should do the same!"

Too late she realized that this had been a diversion and that Brattle was being encouraged, with a few non-too-gentle raps of the cane, to fetch the wine. As the manservant passed Lady Tangle, he inadvertently stepped on one of Lulu's paws, whereupon the animal began to set up an unholy yelping. The bulldog, Reginald, who had taken a strange liking for Lord Failfoot and spent most of his time now hunched beside him, roused himself from a deep slumber and began to growl.

"Filthy little French beast, eh?" the old man declared. "Go after her, boy! Sic! Sic!"

Penelope caught the now-hysterical poodle up in her arms, and Susan could tell by her expression that it was only by dint of making the greatest possible effort that she did not level a retort at her granduncle. Meanwhile Lady Hammerhead appeared to be gritting her teeth, while in her chair in the corner Lady Tangle cast about herself with her fan nervously.

Thus it was that the air was thick with tension when Duggin announced the arrival of their two guests. Having bowed to the ladies, Lord Powell presented his friend, at the same time glancing questioningly at Susan who tried to indicate with a slight shrug of her shoulder that nothing was severely amiss.

"Rhodes, eh?" Lord Failfoot declared, having been put in a more genial mood by the appearance of Brattle bearing the bottle of claret on a tray. "Don't know the name. Still any friend of Powell's is welcome. Bring more glasses, Brattle. No need to drink alone now, what? Its a fine to-do when a fellow has to make a battle plan to get a drink in his own house."

For a moment Susan was afraid that the affronted Lady Hammerhead was about to remind him that it was not his house, but instead she made a graceful flutter about seating everyone, with Penelope, still holding Lulu, positioned beside Lord Powell on the sofa.

"You must not listen to His Lordship," she informed the two young gentlemen, assuming a playful manner. "I only mentioned that, since his gout was bothering him so today, it might be as well if he confined himself to tea."

"Eh, cut the line, madam!" Lord Failfoot shouted. "Cut the line and be done with it. Let a man have a moment's rest from your chatter. Tea indeed! That's a lobcock's drink, damme if it isn't."

Mr. Rhodes, who did not seem at all disconcerted by the old man's attitude, announced that it was his opinion that, while port should be avoided by one in Lord Failfoot's condition, a glass or two of claret could do no harm.

Thus, in a stroke, he won the old man's good will and promptly increased it by telling an amusing story about a fellow barrister who swore that his good health was maintained by the consumption of three bottles of claret a day, with the result that his arguments in court were so involuted that he was often awarded the decision for his client on the basis that neither the judge nor jury could follow his arguments and, as a consequence, concluded that he spoke from the height of a powerful intellect.

Having laughed heartily and imbibed deeply, Lord Failfoot announced that it needed only a glass or two of refreshment and good company to work a cure.

"Mind you, this isn't the usual way of things for me," he confided to James Rhodes, who suddenly might have been the only other person in the room as far as he was concerned. "I'm naught but a lonely old man. The story of my life makes sad hearing, damme if it don't."

Realizing that three glasses of wine which he had consumed rapidly were in danger of causing her granduncle to become maudlin, Susan glanced anxiously at Lord Powell. Certainly it would not suit their purposes if he were to tell James Rhodes about the exile of his only son. Dates might be mentioned and descriptions made. It was not likely, of course, that the young man would draw any relationship between a story of Lord Failfoot's son and his own father, but it was not, she thought, a chance which should be taken. Apparently Lord Powell had reached the same conclusion, for he immediately took the opportunity to mention chess.

"I think you said the other afternoon, sir, that it had been a long time since you enjoyed a game. My friend will forgive me, I know, if I mention that he is a skilled player."

"Why, as for skill, I am not so certain of that,"

121

Mr. Rhodes declared in his unassuming manner, "but if Your Lordship would care to shuffle a few pawns about with me, I should be delighted."

Lord Failfoot responded to the suggestion eagerly, and within a few minutes, he and the young man were facing one another across a board which had been set up by Battle in such a way as to cause the old man the least inconvenience to his gouty leg. As for the others, having been informed by His Lordship that their chatter would do nothing but disturb him, they removed to the other end of the long room where Lord Powell submitted to the blandishments of Penelope and Lady Hammerhead, taking what little opportunity he was allowed to address Lady Tangle and Susan. Only when Penelope betook herself to the pianoforte to regale them with a few songs, her aunt proudly turning the pages for her, did he have an opportunity to speak to Susan in anything which faintly resembled privacy.

"I think," he murmured, "it has gone very well for a start."

"Indeed it has," Susan replied.

She turned to look at the old head and the young bent over the chessboard, the two so close, and closer even than they knew. Turning back, she found Lord Powell's dark eyes waiting for her and, for a moment, she felt a deep content. Granted that the mood was shattered when Penelope began to drum on the keys and Lord Failfoot responded by shouting something about caterwauling and that, as soon as Penelope began to get well into the song, Reginald began to bark and Lulu to whimper; but in the midst of it all Susan realized with a sudden flash of pure happiness that, having come once, the contentment she had felt might well come again.

# Chapter 11

Despite the fact that Lady Hammerhead had assured her time and time again that she was well on the way of capturing Lord Powell's heart, Penelope found that after his second visit she was not as well satisfied as she might be. True that he had been attentive when she talked, and murmured approval at her little concert. True that he had brought Mr. Rhodes with him, presumably to entertain Susan. But that had not been the way of it, and she could not overlook the fact that it was he who had introduced the subject of chess. Surely he could not have forgotten that, on his first visit, her granduncle had professed a fondness for the game. Thus, it could have come as no surprise to him that the old man should demand to play with his friend with the result that Susan had been as much in Lord Powell's company as Penelope had. Indeed, Susan had

125

had the opportunity of speaking privately to him on two occasions, once when Penelope was pausing between songs and again, just before he and Mr. Rhodes had left. True that not many words had been exchanged, but there had been an air of quiet intimacy between the two which Penelope could scarcely account for, and she found herself wondering whether the encounter in the park had been, as Susan claimed, purely accidental.

Determined as she was to win both Lord Powell's and her granduncle's fortune in a single coup, she could afford to ignore nothing and, when she had quizzed her sister to no effect on the evening following Lord Powell's second visit, she set her mind to finding out for certain whether her suspicions were founded on anything more than intuition.

French court circles having been a maze of conspiracy and manipulation, Penelope had learned certain lessons well, one of which being that, if the truth could not be arrived at at the source, it must be achieved, as best one could, at second hand, and it occurred to her that Mr. Rhodes might be able to inform her as to whether there was anything more than the most casual relationship between her sister and Lord Powell.

Next came the question as to when and where she might speak to him privately. Granted that, at her granduncle's urging, Mr. Rhodes had agreed to return for another game of chess shortly, but who knew when that would be? Penelope was too impatient to wait, at any rate. Her aunt had taught her that it was always best to take the initiative and, although she had not confided her suspicions to her guardian, she thought that, were she to have done so, direct action might have been called for. Precisely why she did not go to Lady Hammerhead for advice, Penelope was not certain. Perhaps it was because her aunt lacked a certain delicacy of touch. And this was a delicate matter. No, the best thing was to find the opportunity to talk to Mr. Rhodes alone as soon as possible. What could be more natural than that they should talk of his friend, and when they did, who was to know what invaluable bit of information might be dropped?

If, of course, the young man had been part of the *haut ton,* there would have been no trouble to it, for she would have seen him at any number of entertainments. But, in the general conversation which had preceded his and Lord Powell's departure, she had heard him say, laughingly, that he was quite outside society as befitted a hard-working barrister.

There was only one thing for it, therefore. Penelope must see that he received an invitation to some affair which she intended to attend. Glancing down her list of engagements, she saw that the following evening she and Susan and their aunts were to attend a rout at Lady Plowright's and since Hortense Plowright, the daughter, was a particular friend of hers, nothing could be easier than to send off a note saying that she had recently met a most amusing gentleman and that she hoped, as a special favor to

127

her, he might be added belatedly to the invitation list. Recalling that he had mentioned Lincoln's Inn, Penelope added that a note might find him there, and to guarantee the matter, she had appended a postscript to the effect that Mr. Rhodes was a close friend of Lord Powell's.

Thus it was with considerable satisfaction but little surprise that Penelope came upon the gentleman himself in the Plowrights' green salon on the evening in question. Having previously noticed Lord Powell attending to his sister in one of the other rooms, Penelope found herself in a perfect position to take advantage of the fact that Mr. Rhodes was standing by himself, hands clasped under the tails of his frock coat, watching the other guests with that attitude of open curiosity and general good will which gave him such a boyish quality.

"Miss Collins," he said and then, having bowed, began to flush. "I am afraid," he said, "that I am not certain which Miss Collins I am speaking to."

Although she had not considered masquerading in advance of this meeting, it came to Penelope at once that Mr. Rhodes would speak to her more freely if he thought she were Susan and not Penelope. After all, it was to Susan he had first been introduced, and if, as she suspected, there was some sort of intrigue, she would find out more about it as Susan than as herself.

"So you are not Penelope," Mr. Rhodes said with an easy smile. "If someone had asked me to guess, that would have been the choice I would have made, for no good reason. And see how wrong I would have been."

The young man was clearly delighted to have someone he knew to talk to, and it was the easiest possible accomplishment for Penelope to draw him into one of the alcoves where they could be to themselves and embark on what she intended to appear to be an idle conversation.

Proceeding backward, she spoke at first of how much pleasure her granduncle had taken in what the old man had declared to be the first decent game of chess he had played in years. Flushed with pleasure, Mr. Rhodes explained that he had been taught the game by his own father when he was very young.

"He was, I think, as skilled at it as any man could be," he said, "although it may be that I misremember, since he died when I was only nine."

This not being at all the direction Penelope wished the conversation to take, she had immediately spoken of how kind it had been for Lord Powell to bring him to visit them.

"No doubt he mentioned my granduncle's fondness for chess to you," she suggested. "You were prepared to play?"

But Mr. Rhodes had assured her that that had not been the case.

"I think it was the accidental meeting with you in the park which put the idea into his mind," he said with easy frankness. "Oliver—Lord Powell,

129

that is—has often said that he would like me to know more of his friends than I do. But, of course, he moves in such a different circle that it is not possible. I mean by that that I could not return this sort of hospitality and, as a consequence, prefer to remain on familiar ground. I was quite surprised, in fact, to receive Lady Plowright's invitation, since I have never met either her or her daughter. I would have refused it if Oliver had not urged me to attend. He said that a touch of rarified air once in a while would do me no harm and, no doubt, he is right."

"And how did he explain the invitation?" Penelope asked him guardedly.

Mr. Rhodes smiled at her.

"What was that you said, Miss Collins?" he replied. "You will forgive me, but the exact resemblance between you and your sister quite distracted me for a moment. I caught a glimpse of her in the other room just now as you were speaking, you see, and realized that if you had not asked me if I remembered you and given me your full name as well when we met a few minutes ago, I would not have known which of you I was speaking to."

"Yes, yes, we are much alike," Penelope said impatiently. "But we were speaking of your invitation here this evening. Did Lord Powell speculate as to the reason for it?"

"He thought it must be because Lady Plowright had heard that he and I are particular friends," Mr.

Rhodes told her. "Whatever the reason, I am delighted to be here, for it makes a change."

Given the fact that he was such an easy conversationalist, it was, Penelope thought, astonishing that she was discovering so little. Granted that she now knew that Lord Powell had apparently not brought him to Grosvenor Square with any preconceived notion that he might entertain her granduncle. And Susan's explanation that her meeting with the two gentlemen in the park was accidental seemed to be confirmed. But she wanted further assurance that there was nothing between Lord Powell and her sister and she went after it accordingly.

"Your friend is older than you, I think," she went on. "Is it not strange that he has managed to avoid the wedded state for so long? But then, perhaps, there is some special lady . . ."

Ordinarily she did not care to be quite so direct, but with a gentleman like Mr. Rhodes it seemed necessary. And, indeed, he did not seem surprised by the question.

"I have often twitted him about his remaining quite so long a bachelor," he told her, accompanying the comment with his ready smile. "Perhaps it is because there was only my mother and myself that I put such stock in family. Lord Powell does not feel the lack, of course, with his mother and sister and generations of relatives to look back on. As for me, I have the misfortune not even to know who my father's father was. There was some quarrel, I believe. It must have been that, for my mother often told me that he would not speak about his past, even to her, although he once mentioned Yorkshire and the moors as he remembered them as a boy."

Penelope's first reaction to this recital was one of impatience. Why did the man insist on telling her so much of himself, when all she wanted to know was about Susan and Lord Powell? And then, quite suddenly, his mention of Yorkshire gave her pause. Was it simply coincidence that his father should have come from the same county in which her grandfather lived?

Penelope's thoughts always took a rapid course, but never more rapid than now. Lady Hammerhead liked gossip in almost exact inverse proportion to Lady Tangle, and Penelope had been kept well acquainted with scandals both in and out of the family. As a consequence the details of Lord Failfoot's earlier life came directly to mind, spurred by the unconscious relationship she had drawn by Mr. Rhodes's having mentioned that he did not know his ancestors and that he thought his father must have quarreled with them. And yet, she told herself, it was absurd. It could not be true. Pray God, it must not be true!

Mr. Rhodes, having taken her silence as proof that she was interested in his story—as, indeed, she was, although not in the way he thought—now proceeded to explain that his mother had told him, after her husband's death, that she had often tried to persuade him to tell her something of his past.

"She said," Mr. Rhodes continued earnestly,

132

"that when she questioned him, he became so distraught and angry that she was certain that some past terrible dispute must lie behind it."

"But—but after your father died," Penelope said, "there must have been papers."

"Nothing," Mr. Rhodes told her. "My mother and I questioned his solicitor closely, but all that he would say was that he had been directed to inform my father's family of his death, but that we were to choose his place of burial, for he had left strict orders that it would not be in any family plot."

In an effort to disguise the intensity of her own interest, Penelope murmured something about its being so romantic and mysterious.

"I have only thought of it as being tragic," Mr. Rhodes said slowly. "Of course, he provided for us. We did not lack for anything, and there was money enough to provide me with the training for barrister. But, I tell you frankly, I have always felt the lack of roots."

"And yet you know there is a family somewhere," Penelope said quickly. Her greatest fear now was that they might be interrupted before he could tell her everything she wanted to know. "Have you made no attempt to find them?"

"There are no clues to go on," the young man replied simply. "No clues at all."

Penelope beat the palms of her hands together impatiently and saw him glance at her curiously. She knew that she was showing too much interest, even in a "romantic" story, but she could not stop now.

"Tell me," she said, keeping her voice as even as she could. "In what year did your father die?"

And all the time her mind was working more and more rapidly. Lord Failfoot's son had been disinherited thirty years ago. She was certain of it.

"Why, he died in 1780," Mr. Rhodes said, clearly puzzled now. "In June of that year. But why do you ask, Miss Collins?"

Penelope disregarded the question.

"And what was his Christian name?" she demanded.

"James," Mr. Rhodes replied. "The same as mine."

It was her granduncle's name! The coincidences were too many to be ignored! She felt the blood drain from her face, and the room seemed to whirl around her.

"It is only the heat," she murmured, as Mr. Rhodes quickly led her to a chair. "I shall be all right presently."

"Can I fetch your aunt?" he asked anxiously.

"No! But perhaps a glass of punch . . ."

She needed to be alone. To think. It could not be happenstance that this young man, out of all of London, should have been the very one to have been brought to meet her granduncle. Brought by Lord Powell. After both had met Susan in the park. Susan, who wanted nothing to do with the old man's fortune. Susan, who would be delighted if Lord Failfoot could be united with an heir.

It came as a certainty to Penelope that James Rhodes *was* that heir, and that Lord Powell and her sister had schemed to ingratiate him with his grandfather. The young man himself knew nothing. He would have had to be a great actor to have pretended to know nothing so convincingly. And he must be kept from ever knowing. Or, if that were impossible to prevent, Lord Failfoot must learn to hate him as well and truly as he he had hated his son.

Instantly a plan came, half-formulated, to her mind. When Mr. Rhodes returned with the glass of punch, Penelope gave every appearance of being quite herself again. And then she spent the next hour of the evening practicing every art she knew to convince the bewildered young man that he was quite the most fascinating gentleman she had ever met. By the time they had danced a waltz, Mr. Rhodes could not fail to realize that Miss Susan Collins had taken a very great fancy to him indeed.

# Chapter 12

Lord Powell had meant to keep his friend James close company that evening, since he knew that he would be among strangers, for the most part. But it so happened that his sister Evelyn, having quarreled with her beau, was in a nervous and excited state and, as a consequence, demanded his attention. Thus it was that he was not even certain that James had honored his invitation to the ball, having been required to see that Evelyn was provided with partners. This was frustration enough in itself, but even more annoying was the fact that he did not have the opportunity to speak with Susan Collins, although he saw her—or perhaps it was Penelope—on the dance floor.

It was a great annoyance to Lord Powell that, at a distance, he could not tell the difference between the two sisters. He was certain, of course, that in a direct encounter he could not be deceived, but it stung him to the quick to be forced to see a golden-haired beauty waltzing past him and not be certain whether it was Susan or Penelope. Having seen them enter the ballroom with their aunts, he was aware that they had chosen to dress alike in simple white muslin ball gowns, and so no difference in dress could give him a clue as to which was which. And yet he determined, once his sister was in a calmer state, to seek out Susan to inquire as to the impression James had made on Lord Failfoot.

True, his hopes were high. The old gentleman had certainly enjoyed his game of chess enough to ask James to make a quick return to the house on Grosvenor Square. But it was essential to him that Susan tell him herself how strong the favorable impression had been. It would be a fine thing if James could be united with his grandfather and become his heir, not only to the title, but to the estate as well.

At the first interval, having had the satisfaction of seeing Evelyn led off to the punch table by a young gentleman who seemed well able to provide her with some distraction, Lord Powell began to search for Susan and found, instead, Penelope waiting at his elbow.

It was strange, he thought, what a difference there was between the two sisters as soon as one was close enough to see their eyes, to hear their voices. Perhaps it was because there was a certain disquiet about Penelope which struck his sensibility at once. At all events, he reluctantly resigned himself to her attentions, agreeing that his second visit to her granduncle had been a success and that much thanks for that were due to Mr. Rhodes.

"My sister was much struck by your friend," Penelope told him. "Indeed, they have been talking together for ever so long in the green salon. How clever of you to have guessed that they would like one another so much."

The idea came as a considerable shock to Lord Powell, although he hid it well enough. The last thing in his mind had been that James would find Susan appealing, although, now that he thought of it, what could have been more natural. This unexpected turn of events troubled him, and he could only hope that Penelope exaggerated.

In the meantime the gentleman in question, having been told by Penelope that he should rejoin her as soon as she had tidied her hair, watched Susan descending from the upper rooms which had been set aside for the ladies and moved quickly to greet her as she reached the bottom stair. Unaccustomed to flirtation as he was, he had been considerably flattered by the attention which he imagined she had paid to him for the past hour, and it was, as a consequence, that he greeted her with the utmost informality, offering his arm and smiling broadly.

"Why, Mr. Rhodes," Susan declared. "How nice it is to see you here."

Although by "here" she meant the ball in general, James took her to mean that she had not expected him to be waiting at the foot of the staircase.

"But of course I was waiting," he told her. "How good it is of you to make me feel so much at home among the *haut ton*. May I ask for the next waltz?"

Such an air of intimacy took Susan quite by surprise, but, because she liked him and because she had a considerable interest in his future, she agreed at once to dance with him once the next set began. And yet she thought it very strange that he should treat her as though they were old friends. And, as for thanking her for making him feel "at home," what had she done except to descend a flight of stairs and smile at him?

Certainly, if Mr. Rhodes had mentioned their past conversation, Susan would have guessed that a deceit had been practiced on him. But Penelope, quite wisely, before taking leave of him, had made him promise that they would make no reference to what had been spoken between them for the remainder of the evening.

"It makes me feel too sad," she had told him, "to think that you should know nothing of your family. We will speak of it another time, but for the present it will be best to pretend that our tête-à-tête had never taken place."

And so, although it still troubled Mr. Rhodes to know why she had taken such an interest in his family, he said not a word about it, and, in a moment, the orchestra having struck up their music once again, he and Susan took the floor and he with

140

no clue as to the exchange which had been made except that she seemed to float more lightly in his arms than she had before.

When the waltz was finished, he made no move to return her to where Lady Tangle sat in the corner. Instead, he assumed a proprietorial air which took Susan greatly by surprise and dismayed her not a little, since she so wanted to have a word or two in private with Lord Powell.

"Another glass of punch will do you good," he assured her, leading her to the table. "Although, I must say, that your color has quite returned."

Susan was too puzzled by this remark to ask why it had been made. It was possible, of course, that he had thought that she seemed pale when she had been dancing previously with Lord Owens. Indeed, that must be the answer. And, because he was obviously so eager to please, she took his arm.

His next remark astonished her even more.

"I did not have an opportunity to speak at length to your sister the other afternoon," he said, "but I am delighted that she and Oliver take such an interest in one another. I have long urged him to marry and I am certain that it will make a great match."

Susan almost let her glass of punch fall to the floor.

"You speak of Lord Powell, sir?" she asked. "Lord Powell and Penelope?"

"But, of course," he assumed her. "See how closely they are talking together at the other end of the room. If she shares your grace, which I am certain that she does, she should make him very happy indeed. And it is high time that he found someone, as I have often told him."

Penelope and Lord Powell! Penelope and Oliver! How on earth had Mr. Rhodes come to think of such a thing? Susan wondered. With an awful rush it came to her that there was only one way that he could have conceived such a notion. Lord Powell must have told him that he was attracted to her sister!

Was it possible? Had she deceived herself in thinking that simply because Lord Powell had signed a note to her with his Christian name and because they were both involved in an intrigue to gain Mr. Rhodes his rightful heritage that there was a special closeness between them? He had treated her as a friend in whom he could confide, certainly, but had he, all the while, been increasingly attracted to her sister?

A glance across the floor assured her that Mr. Rhodes had spoken correctly when he had said that Penelope and Lord Powell were deep in conversation with one another. Good Lord, how blind she must have been to think that he saw Penelope as she did. He had been taken in, for all his sophistication. Once she had been prepared to tell him of her granduncle's scheme, but now it was too late. If he were, indeed, truly attracted to Penelope, that must serve.

"I think you are looking pale again," Miss Susan," Mr. Rhodes announced. "Come. Take a seat here and I will stand here beside you. Let me open this window a bit to let in the breeze."

His attentiveness could not be idly dismissed, and Susan submitted to the attention, disguising her distress. She could not bear to question him as to how and why he had reached the conclusion that Lord Powell was romantically interested in her sister. And so she took refuge in small talk, most of which involved her granduncle.

"He is an extraordinary old gentleman," Mr. Rhodes assured her. "And it is strange, you know. Although I had never met him before, he reminded me of someone. I have been searching my mind to think of who it is, with no success. And yet, when I was at chess with him, I had the most amazing sense of *déjà vu*. I felt, somehow, as though I had known him before. And I was quite comfortable with him in an odd sort of way."

"Then you must visit him again," Susan said, determined to seem quite calm, quite collected. "Come as often as you like. Your visits will do him good."

And, all the time, she was thinking that, even though Lord Powell had, apparently, been captivated by her sister, she must attend to the main concern, which was to make such friends of this young man and Lord Failfoot as to insure that, when the truth of their relationship was told, both would accept it gladly.

And, even as she spoke, Lord Powell, on the other side of the room with the persistent Penelope

143

still in tow, noted the seriousness of their conversation and thought that Penelope must indeed be correct in saying that the two were attracted to one another. What an irony it was, he told himself as Penelope chattered on about this and that, that in the interest of doing his friend a good service, he would have risked his own happiness.

It was not until the third interval that, having released himself from Penelope with the excuse of having to look after his sister, Lord Powell encountered his friend alone, Susan having made her escape from his attentions by saying that she must see that her aunt was comfortable and well entertained.

"I am pleased to see that you have been enjoying yourself, James," he said. "Miss Susan Collins is a delightful companion, is she not?"

There was a certain stiffness in Lord Powell's voice which gave James Rhodes pause. Never before had he seen his friend look at him in such a guarded manner. But his frankness did not desert him. After all, it was Oliver who had introduced him to the beauty, and he wished, above all things, to thank him. It was not that he had fallen instantly in love. That would never be his way. But he felt as gratified as any gentleman must do at being the center of a lovely young lady's interest, albeit granted that she had seemed so much more flirtatious before the first interval when they had talked so intimately in the green salon.

"Miss Susan has been very kind," he admitted. "Indeed, I have spent the entire evening with her.

144

We began with a long talk, and afterward she showed no interest in dividing her attention. How can I think you, Oliver, for urging me to attend this evening."

And, although Lord Powell smiled and offered his congratulations, there was something in his manner which gave James Rhodes pause.

"If you have been well entertained, I am glad enough for it," his friend replied. "And it stands as a matter of course that you must visit her again as soon as possible. But now, I think, I will cut the evening short. My sister is, I think, exhausted. Goodbye for now, my friend. I wish you well."

# Chapter 13

Penelope was so well pleased with her evening's work that she decided, the next morning, to take Lady Hammerhead into her confidence. After all, her aunt was certain to be pleased that she had been so clever, first in detecting the real reason that Mr. Rhodes had been introduced into their household and recognizing, as a consequence, that Lord Powell and Susan might well have had private dealings. And, as if that were not enough, had she not set the stage to foil their plan? Penelope stretched luxuriously in her canopied bed and reflected that there was more scheming to be done if she were, at one and the same time, to put an end to Mr. Rhodes's chances and keep Lord Powell's regard, as well.

As soon as she thought it possible that her aunt might be awake, Penelope wrapped a pink silk dressing gown about her and hurried down the hall to knock at Lady Hammerhead's door, reflecting as she did so the absurdity of having her bedchamber adjoin Susan's and not her aunt's. Of course the arrangement had been made in the anticipation that the sisters would be close. And what a far-flung notion that had been! If she was right in her conjectures, Susan had taken part in a plot which would have removed her granduncle's fortune from her grasp forever. She would, Penelope thought, take considerable pains to see that the scheme which was unfolding at the back of her mind include some detail which would spell disaster for her twin. It was, after all, no more than Susan deserved.

Lady Hammerhead was not at her very best in the morning, inclined to be more disagreeable than usual, more easily put out. One of the reasons for her low mood was the fact that morning light is notoriously unkind to ladies of a certain age, and as a consequence, Penelope was not surprised to find her with the curtains of her chamber drawn against the sun in which dimness Lady Hammerhead found it possible to approach her mirror before which she now sat, applying vermillion to her cheeks with practiced fingers.

When Penelope had told her story, Lady Hammerhead sat very still indeed, still staring into her mirror. Even in the dusky light it was apparent that she no longer needed vermillion to stain her cheeks. A vein in her forehead bulged alarmingly, and she was breathing like one who had just lost a race.

"That chit!" she exclaimed. "With her pert, pretty ways! So good that butter wouldn't melt in her mouth! And all the time bamboozling us!"

She rose and began to pace about the shadowy room, pounding her hands together in her fury. "How did the minx arrange it?" she demanded. "How did she come to know of this man Rhodes? What time has she had for conspiring with Lord Powell? I have been a sapskull not to notice anything! Why, when she talked about not wanting the money, I thought it was a conceit. But now it seems that she was so much in earnest about it that she must seek out the old man's heir! Such spite! Such selfishness! If she did not want to compete with you for Lord Powell, she could simply have stepped aside and left you to him. But no! That would not do for goody-two-shoes! She must see you out of pocket and humiliated, as well. Do you think that she has told him of your granduncle's plans, Penelope? Do you think she has gone that far?"

In her fury and bewilderment, Lady Hammerhead had taken her niece by the shoulders and now, as she asked her question, proceeded to shake her violently.

"Do control yourself, Aunt Lucinda!" Penelope cried, wrenching herself away from those frantic hands. "In the first place, we cannot be certain that Susan arranged anything, let alone told secrets out of this house. I agree with what you say about her. She is too good by far. But we have no indication—not a single one—that she knows Mr.

149

Rhodes's true identity. We cannot even be certain that Lord Powell knows! Indeed, we cannot be absolutely positive that he *is* the old man's grandson."

"But of course he is!" Lady Hammerhead declared emphatically. "The moment that you suggested it, I saw it must be true. The name's the same. The death's in the same year and month. The secrecy. It is a rare man, even in London, who does not know something about his father's family. And, more than that, I can see the resemblance, now that my attention has been brought to bear on it. There is the same cast about the chin and mouth, and the noses might as well be identical."

"You knew granduncle's son, then?"

"He was my first cousin." Lady Hammerhead declared irritatedly. "Of course I never set eyes on him once he had broken with his father, but I knew him when he was the age that Mr. Rhodes is now, and I assure you, the resemblance is quite startling. It explains, of course, why he seemed so familiar to me, although I cannot be blamed for not making the connection, since it has been a good many years since I saw his father."

They had set a seal on that, then, Penelope thought with satisfaction. One point made, and now the next which was to determine whether his having been brought to this house was accidental or planned and, if planned, by whom.

"I do not think it could have been coincidence," Lady Hammerhead said firmly, parading up and down the dusky room, a storklike figure in her bro-

150

cade dressing gown which settled about her like folded wings, allowing her thin neck and beakish nose to complete the parallel. "Life is full of them, no doubt, but I have found that this is most frequently true with the small things—the incidentals. And this matter of a reappearing heir is not one of those."

Having already made up her mind that, coincidence or not, it should not be treated as though it were, Penelope listened to her aunt with half a mind, the other half being preoccupied with a scheme which, in a moment, would, she thought, burst full-formed and phoenixlike into her mind.

"Now, as for the part your sister has played," Lady Hammerhead went on, "I do not think she could have instigated anything, since she knows no one in London. I mean by that that, although she has acquaintances, she would have had no way of meeting someone like Mr. Rhodes if he had not been presented to her."

"And who but Lord Powell could have presented him?" Penelope mused, coiling herself on the chaise longue at the foot of the bed.

"Precisely!" her aunt exclaimed. "But how could he have known of the connection?"

She paused mid-progress and clapped her hands, which seemed more talonlike than usual without their usual burden of rings.

"Of course!" she cried. "Lord Powell's grandfather must be the connecting link. He knew your granduncle when they were young. He must have known that the son had been disinherited. Perhaps he saw him here in London or elsewhere. Knew the new name he had taken. He must have told his grandson. What could have been more natural than that Lord Powell, as a consequence, would take an interest in James Rhodes? It explains their friendship, no doubt."

She turned to glare at Penelope. "You say that you are all but certain that young Rhodes is ignorant of his relationship with Lord Failfoot?"

"He is not subtle enough to make such an effective pretense of ignorance of the matter," Penelope assured her. "Remember that when he talked to me, he thought I was Susan. If he had been part of the conspiracy, he would have made quite another conversation, surely."

"Yes, you are right in that," her aunt said reflectively. "Then what must we assume? That Lord Powell and Susan wish to have him ingratiate himself with the old man. Once the two are friends, they will make the announcement. But, then again, where will be their proof?"

"No doubt the legal firm which handled Mr. Rhodes's father's affairs would provide it once they could see the importance of doing so," Penelope said distractedly, her mind still busy with her scheme. "After all, their former client is dead, and there is the matter of the title. Legally Mr. Rhodes cannot be kept from that."

"Ah, but he must be kept from receiving the inheritance," Lady Hammerhead said shrilly. "Fail-foot must be kept to his original plan."

"And yet even if he could be kept to it, there are difficulties," Penelope told her. "If Lord Powell is as set as he must be, given what he has done, on re-instating his friend, he would have no part in divert-ing the fortune to me."

"Then what is to be done?" Lady Hammerhead wailed, pressing her hands to her forehead.

"Two things are of the first importance," Penel-ope said, rising from the lounge, her manner now as crisp as her voice. "I have been thinking of it and I can see the solution."

"Ah, but you are a clever girl!" her aunt ex-claimed, embracing. "Come! Tell me what you mean."

"First, I must see to it that Lord Powell is safe from Susan's snares," Penelope announced. "Pah, I cannot stand these shadows!"

Her aunt watched her draw the curtains back with only a murmured protest. In the clear daylight her uncompleted toilette was all too apparent, but she kept her eyes trained on her niece.

"I have already taken the first step in that direc-tion," Penelope said firmly. "No doubt Mr. Rhodes will have told Lord Powell of the attentions I paid to him last night. Remember he thinks he spoke so intimately with Susan, and he must believe that she is very interested in him. If anything has passed be-tween her and Lord Powell, he must believe that

153

she is capable of romantic duplicity. I can do more to convince him of it. But, of that later."

"How well you have learned all the little lessons I taught you, my dear," Lady Hammerhead said admiringly.

The sunlight made a golden halo of Penelope's hair, but the expression on her face was far from angelic.

"The next thing to be accomplished is that Lord Failfoot be given some cause for mistrusting Mr. Rhodes," the girl went on. "Some barrier must be put in the way of his ever accepting him as heir, even when he knows the truth. And I believe Aunt, that in a single move I can accomplish both aims. Yes, I am certain of it!"

Sitting down at the rosewood escritoire in the corner, she took out a piece of stationery and dipped a quill pen in the ink. For a moment she paused as though lost in thought and then began to scribble hurriedly as though fearful of losing an inspiration. Lady Hammerhead began a question, but the girl silenced her with an impatient wave of her hand.

It was not Lady Hammerhead's way to sit quietly and wait, but this time she did. Not a sound was heard in the room except the ticking of the clock and the scratch of the pen until Penelope finally pushed her chair from the desk and offered the paper on which she had been writing to her aunt.

Lady Hammerhead began to read it eagerly and

then broke off and looked at her niece in bewilderment.

"But this is a love letter!" she cried. "At least it comes very close to being. What good will be served by your submitting such sentiments to Mr. Rhodes? He will think you are mad!"

Penelope's smile was smooth and silky.

"Do look at the signature before you read further, Aunt Lucinda," she said in a voice which would have melted butter.

Lady Hammerhead turned the sheet and did as she was told.

"But you have signed your sister's name!" she exclaimed. "What good do you hope to come from this, pray?"

"You are not chiding me, I hope, Aunt," Penelope said sharply. "If you are, I will regret that I made you privy to my plans."

"No, no. Of course I do not chide," Lady Hammerhead said plaintively. "It is only that I do not understand what you hope to accomplish."

"Why, only that Mr. Rhodes may be brought to respond in kind," Penelope said slyly. "The letter can easily be intercepted if one is expecting it, which Susan will not be."

"Leaving you in possession of a warm letter addressed to her!" Lady Hammerhead said, all bewilderment. "And what would you do with it, pray?"

"I think," Penelope said slowly, "that you can safely leave that to me, Aunt. I assure you that I know very well what I am doing."

# Chapter 14

At ten o'clock that morning a messenger left the house on Grosvenor Square. He returned with no reply, which was to be expected. At two that afternoon a boy hired off the streets, an engaging urchin with a jacket four times too big for him and a hat of proportionate measurements, appeared with two messages. Placing both on a silver salver, the footman took the first to Lord Failfoot in the library. Returning to the hallway, the young man found Miss Penelope Collins waiting for him.

"Is that letter for my sister?" she demanded. "Ah, yes, I see that it is. She has been expecting it."

And lifting the missive from the salver, she hurried up the stairs, leaving the footman to shrug his shoulders and go off through the green baize door to the servants' quarters where cook was keeping a pot of tea warm for him.

Lady Hammerhead was waiting for Penelope in her private sitting room upstairs, a seething mass of excitement.

"Let me see it, my dear!" she cried when her niece hurried into the room, already cutting the seal with her fingernails. "Pray, hurry, do! If he has put her off, we have lose the game!"

Penelope's dark eyes skimmed the page which was covered from top to bottom with exquisitely formed letters written very small. "All is well!" she announced triumphantly. "I can see at once that this is precisely the sort of thing I wanted. He does not announce for her, of course. It is too soon for that. But he is flattered and he does us the goodness of quoting some of 'Susan's' more graceful declarations. All the better, that. The old man will see—or think he sees—that, far from playing the game he set for us, Susan has been intriguing under his very nose."

"But Mr. Rhodes's tone, my dear!" Lady Hammerhead demanded, making futile grabs for the letter which Penelope seemed to see fit to keep in her possession. "His tone is all, I think."

"It is precisely as it should be," Penelope assured her. "He does not take too many liberties. Indeed, knowing what you and I know, his astonishment at having received such a message is apparent. But to the old man it will only seem to be the intimate sort of message which passes between lovers. La, the fellow writes rather well. See how he speaks of her

158

hair as a gold coronet. And the magic in her eyes. Ah, yes. Ah, yes."

"Let me read the letter, do, my dear!" Lady Hammerhead declared, clearly not at all satisfied by the peek at particular passages which she had been allowed.

"Later, I think," Penelope said. "Mr. Rhodes speaks, you see, of coming here this afternoon. He says that he has written Lord Failfoot a note announcing that intention. It will be best if I get to the old skip-brain before Mr. Rhodes arrives. If I handle the matter well enough, I can assure him of quite a different reception from that which he so clearly expects."

Hurrying downstairs to the library, Penelope interrupted her granduncle in the midst of requesting Brattle to fetch him some champagne.

"I have a fancy for it," he said half-defiantly to his grandniece when he saw that she had overheard the order. "My leg gives me a deal of pain today, my dear, indeed it does."

"But, sir, you had not mentioned that before," Brattle declared. "Why, it's a fact that you told me not five minutes ago that it felt as well as ever it had in months."

"Pah!" Lord Failfoot bellowed, puffing out a great breath like an angry thundercloud. "Why, I was simply putting a brave face on things, you cullskap! Out and about for that champagne before I clout you good and proper."

Brattle ducked with a show of considerable expertize as the old man whirled his cane about his head, and hurried to the door where he made pause for a moment beside Penelope, who kept the knob a captive.

"Find some excuse to delay bringing that bottle for as long as possible," she whispered. "It may be that I will be able to distract him sufficiently, so that he will forget he ever ordered it. You know how bad it is for him."

Brattle inclined his head respectfully, and Penelope prepared to glide across the room. It was always best, she thought, to make an effective entrance, even in this case when her granduncle had chosen to turn his attention to the bulldog, Reginald, to whom he was chatting sotto voce. Still, she had been clever in intercepting Brattle. The longer the old man was forced to wait for his bottle, the more rapidly his good temper would disintegrate. Nothing would suit better than that he been in an edgy mood by the time she had delivered her news, and well Penelope knew it.

And so she hedged a bit, wanting the impatience for the delayed bottle to set in before she came directly to the point.

"Are you expecting Mr. Rhodes, sir?" she asked innocently, pointing at the chess table which had been drawn up before the fire, it being a damp and chilly day.

"I am, indeed," the old gentleman said, patting Reginald's head until the bulldog buried his muzzle between his paws and began to snore happily.

There was a long pause during which Lord Failfoot whistled a little tune between his teeth and kept time by thumping his cane against one leg of the chair. As usual, he did not encourage small talk.

"Won't want anyone looking on, Mr. Rhodes and me," the old man said finally. "Splendid young fellow, that. Something familiar about him. Odd thing. He tells me he's never been in Yorkshire and I haven't left the place for thirty years until now. It's a puzzle, that. Damn that Brattle. Where's my champagne?"

"I find it very interesting, sir," Penelope said, seeing that the time to speak had come at last, "that you should believe that Mr. Rhodes is coming here for the express purpose of playing chess with you."

"What's that?" Lord Failfoot roared. "There's a mean edge to your voice, gel. Hinting at something, are you? Spit it out and get it over with, that's my motto. What other reason would the fellow have for coming here?"

Penelope cleared her throat and assumed a very proper expression.

"I think, perhaps, sir, you should read this letter." she said in a low voice, handing it to him. "It will provide a better explanation than I can give you of certain . . ."

"Damme, this letter isn't for me!" the old man exploded. "Can't you read, gel. It's not for me or for you either. 'My dear Susan.' That's what it says.

Perhaps you'd like to tell me what we're doing with your sister's private correspondence."

Penelope tried not to appear taken aback. After all, she had come prepared to tack and shift according to whatever wind was blowing.

"It was delivered to me quite accidentally, sir," she said. "And since it never entered my head that it was for anyone else, I did not even look at the salutation until I was well into the letter . . . and then, of course, I was so appalled that anyone would have the audacity to address me in such a bold manner that I paused and . . . well, saw that it was not for me at all."

"Bold manner, eh?" Lord Failfoot declared. "Audacity, eh? Shocked you, did it. Take a deal to do that, I think, my little pretty."

"I was shocked," Penelope protested. "Susan has kept this all quite secret and I thought—I thought that you should know what she has been up to."

"More than you have, I'll be bound," he told her, with a sneer. "Pity you've lacked the opportunity, my gel. Come to the point. Has she got Powell to the point of making a declaration? Is that what's galling you?"

This was not precisely the sort of response which Penelope had wished to engender, and it made her wary. After all, the old man was no innocent and probably two steps ahead of her in reading character. She determined not to make the mistake of attempting to deceive him as to her own motives, although she would not go so far as to tell him the real truth about how the letter had come into her hands.

"If this letter were from Lord Powell, it would more than gall me, sir," she replied boldly. "But the fact is that it comes from Mr. James Rhodes."

"Rhodes! What's that, eh?" the old gentleman demanded, thumping his cane with such force that Reginald roused and began to growl. "Why, she scarcely knows the fellow! And, besides, he comes here to play chess with me."

"That is just the point, sir," Penelope said eagerly. "He only pretends to want to amuse you. There is no harm in his courting Susan, of course, but he should not be a hypocrite about the reason for his coming to this house. I knew that you would feel that, as I do."

"I do not like a fellow who is all corners," Lord Failfoot said petulantly. "Pretends to enjoy my company, does he, and all because he wants a glance of your sister, who may or may not have encouraged him, gels being what they are."

"Oh, if you were to read this letter carefully you would see that she must have encouraged him a very great deal," Penelope said quickly. "Indeed, there are certain references to phrases which she has written to him previously which I believe you would find most shocking and . . ."

"How do you know what I will find if I read this carefully, chit?" Lord Failfoot demanded. "Why not a moment ago you assured me that you had only skimmed the start of it. Oh, never mind! I would have done the same, I expect, when I was your age. And would do now if my eyes were not so rheumy."

For a moment he leered at her conspiratorily and then brought up the question of the champagne, which still had not appeared, adding that Brattle was an addlepate and something worse, the exact nature of which Penelope did not catch.

"But, Uncle, are you not annoyed with Mr. Rhodes?" she protested.

"I am more put out with Brattle at the moment," Lord Failfoot assured her. "Here, what's the reason you should want me to be in a temper with Rhodes, as well?"

Penelope knew that she must walk a very narrow line here. Clearly the old man would never believe that she had only his best interest at heart. The mistrust in human nature which had kept him so long a recluse must extend to her as well.

"The fact is, sir," she said, determined to let him know all at once, "that Mr. Rhodes is guilty of more than the one deceit I mentioned. He is your grandson, sir. If you accost him with the fact, he will deny knowledge of it. But it is true and he knows it. And so does Susan. The two have schemed to have him ingratiate himself with you in order that you will restore the natural line of inheritance. That is why my sister has been so disinclined to pursue Lord Powell. She wants to have the man she loves and your fortune to boot. And I, for one, am disinclined to let her oblige herself!"

# Chapter 15

When Penelope came to tell Susan that their grand-uncle wanted to see her in the library at once, there was something in her eyes, some little glitter of triumph that gave Susan warning. And yet she could not think what might have happened. She had been disappointed, the night before, not to have had an opportunity to talk to Lord Powell, particularly since they had so much to discuss. But it had been clear that he had been preoccupied with his sister for the first half of the evening, and for the remainder, Mr. Rhodes had been so persistent that she had seen no way of escaping him. Indeed, he had made her exceedingly uncomfortable finally, partly because he seemed to assume that she would dance every dance with him and partly for some other reason which, even now, she could not put her finger on.

Still, she was glad now that she had been friendly to him. After all, he was her cousin, even though he did not know it and, as she kept reminding herself, he must have felt quite lost in the company of so many strangers. Besides, he was such a pleasant fellow, always so eager to please and with a real knack of telling stories that the hours had passed easily enough. As for Lord Powell, as soon as his sister was settled with dancing partners, he had been monopolized by Penelope completely. Perhaps, Susan thought now, that was why her sister looked so self-satisfied.

Susan was not quite sure what troubled her. Perhaps it was because she had received no letter from Lord Powell that morning. She had been more certain than she should have been, perhaps, that he would write to her to arrange to bring Mr. Rhodes for another visit. The young man's first encounter with Lord Failfoot had gone so swimmingly that surely he should come again as soon as possible.

But, as she followed Penelope down the long corridor to the stairs, Susan told herself that Lord Powell must have other demands on his time. Even though he was currently in London, there must be estate affairs to be seen to, letters to write and business to conduct. Or it might be that his mother's condition had worsened. Or perhaps it was simply that his sister Evelyn needed his attention, since it seemed clear, from what Susan had observed, that something had gone wrong between her and the bland-faced young man she had gone off with so gaily on the evening of Lady Winsome's entertainment.

Whatever the answer to his delay in contacting her, she knew that she would hear from him soon, if for no other reason than that he knew, as well as she, how important it was that Mr. Rhodes and his grandfather be brought together.

With these thoughts running through her mind, Susan found herself quite at a loss when, having entered the library, she found quite a company assembled. Lady Tangle sat in a corner looking very hot and bothered and twirling her fan frantically, while Lady Hammerhead wandered about the room with an air of great excitement. Lulu and Reginald sat facing one another on either side of the fireplace, clearly in a mood to do battle, should the opportunity present itself. And, just inside the door and to the side, Mr. Rhodes stood stiff and ill at ease, his shoulders very square under the blue superfine of his jacket. His face lit up when Susan entered the room, as though, in coming, she had brought an answer to some pressing matter.

And, indeed, something was very wrong. The air itself seemed to be thick with trouble brewing. One look at her granduncle assured Susan that such was the case, for there was a look of malice on his face as he peered up at her from his chair, which was enough to shake her.

"Now, chit!" he demanded. "We will have all this settled once and for all! What have you been up to, eh? Is what your sister tells me true? No dammed hemming and hawing, if you please! A simple yes or no will do!"

"Since I do not know what she has told you, I cannot possibly answer your question," Susan said, trying to keep her voice even.

"Twiddle-twaddle!" Lord Failfoot bellowed, banging his cane on the floor. "You and this—this fellow have been scheming to get my money! Simple as that! Tell me yes or no. Mind, I am in no mood for Banbury stories!"

"It seems you have been told one, none the less," Susan declared, her own temper flaring. "If by 'this fellow' you mean Mr. Rhodes, I can assure you that we have never plotted anything."

Lord Failfoot's wrinkled throat reared from his cravat like a turtle's rising from its shell. His beady eyes sparkled with rage, and once again, he drummed with his cane on the floor.

"You deny that you have exchanged love letters with him, eh? You dare to deny that when I have the evidence in my hand?"

He waved a sheet of paper at her. Stepping forward, Susan took it from him and scanned it quickly.

"I have never seen this letter before," she said. "Neither can I believe that Mr. Rhodes wrote it, since I have given him no encouragement to address me in such a manner. It is a forgery, I assure you."

"I am afraid that it is not," Mr. Rhodes said, coming to stand beside her. "But I would never

168

have written it if I had not received your letter this morning. I do not want to speak out of place, but it seems that something is very wrong here, and I do not understand my part in it."

"Jackanapes!" Lord Failfoot shouted. "Gudgeon!"

"I do not know whether you are addressing me or Mr. Rhodes, sir," Susan said angrily. "But, I advise you that I do not believe that either one of us should be spoken to in such a manner. I quite agree with Mr. Rhodes that the truth should be told and I am sorry that he should have been led to write this letter by someone who clearly wishes to do him harm."

She turned and looked speculatively at Penelope, who stared back at her defiantly.

"I wrote no letter to Mr. Rhodes," Susan went on. "Clearly, however, someone did in an attempt to make him reply as he has done."

"What sort of nonsense is this?" Lord Failfoot began. "Damme, I tell you . . ."

"And I tell you that you, too, have been misled, sir," Susan interrupted. "Tell me, Mr. Rhodes, were you surprised to receive a letter with my name attached?"

"Indeed I was, Miss Collins," the young man replied. "Of course I appreciated your friendliness last evening, but even so . . ."

"And when was it last evening that I was at my most intimate with you?" Susan asked him. "Was it, perhaps, before the first interval?"

"Yes, it was then," he told her. "You will remember that you led me to speak of my father."

Susan's eyes narrowed as she glanced a second time at Penelope.

"And would it surprise you, Mr. Rhodes," she went on, "to learn that during the time before the first interval I was engaged in dancing with Lord Wilfred Owens and with others who will, if necessary, be more than willing to confirm the fact?"

"But you said that you were Susan," Mr. Rhodes protested. "It must have been you unless . . ."

Realization dawned on his face, and now it was his turn to stare at Penelope who, having picked up Lulu, was pressing her face against the poodle's curly white back.

"Surely you are not attempting to pluck yourself out of a hole you have fallen into by accusing your sister of deliberate deceit!" Lady Hammerhead exclaimed. "Why, it is just as I thought. You will stop at nothing."

"Stubble it, woman!" Lord Failfoot roared. "Is this true, jade! Come. Leave that dog alone and tell me. Did you write to this fellow and pretend to be your sister? Did you pretend the night before?"

"If—if I did, sir," Penelope said breathlessly, "it was because . . . because . . ."

"It was because you wished to turn our grand-uncle against him," Susan declared.

"Why should I have not?" Penelope demanded. "You may not have written to Mr. Rhodes, but you have schemed in his favor."

170

Mr. Rhodes looked from one girl to the other in obvious bewilderment.

"Favor?" he muttered. "What possible favor could be done me?"

"Oh, no doubt you will pretend not to know until the last," Penelope said scornfully. "But I know and Susan knows and your dear friend Lord Powell knows just who you really are and what you are after!"

"But I am after nothing," Mr. Rhodes replied, his face gone quite white. "And as for who I am, I know that well enough."

Dropping the poodle, who yelped as he struck the floor, Penelope advanced to face the young man. Lord Failfoot, suddenly gone silent, sat peering at them, his eyes blazing.

"And do you claim, then, that you did not convince Lord Powell to contrive to gain you entry to this house?" Penelope demanded.

Susan started to speak, but Mr. Rhodes raised his hand as though to silence her. It was clear that he was shocked and bewildered, but equally apparent that he intended to respond to the accusations which were being made against him himself.

"Lord Powell brought me here because he considered you his friends and wanted me to meet you," he said simply.

"I find it difficult to believe that he should have chosen to introduce you, quite by accident, to the one man in London who could, if he chose, make you his heir!" Penelope hissed.

Mr. Rhodes drew back as though she had struck him. Even Lady Hammerhead seemed appalled by the force with which Penelope spoke, for she moved toward her niece, murmuring some warning. As for Lady Tangle, Susan saw that she had discarded her fan and had buried her plump face in her hands, peering between the fingers like a frightened child.

"I have no idea what you are talking about, Miss Collins," Mr. Rhodes said in a voice which seemed to come from a great distance.

How Susan blamed herself then for having had any hand in bringing matters to this point. Never had she thought to embarrass and humiliate this young gentleman with his open ways and gentle temperament. But she had never dreamed that Penelope might guess. . . .

"You gave me all the information I needed, sir, before the first interval last evening," her sister was saying. "I have a special knack for putting two and two together, I assure you. It will be as well for you if you cast off your innocent airs. They did not suit Susan and they do not suit you. You knew from the start that you were Lord Failfoot's grandson. Once you had made yourself at home here, caused him to like and trust you, the truth would have come out soon enough. You are only troubled now because it has been told too soon."

She paused, but only, Susan thought, because she was out of breath.

"It is impossible," she heard Mr. Rhodes mur-

mur. His face was even whiter than before, and his hands were clenched at his side. Taking three steps forward, he stood looking down at the old man.

"Tell me it is not so, sir," he said simply.

"Your Christian name?" Lord Failfoot said in an oddly abrupt tone, as though he were a judge interrogating a witness.

"Why, it is James."

"So was my son called. When did your father die?"

Mr. Rhodes named that date and Lord Failfoot nodded dolefully.

"And he told you something of me?"

"He never spoke of the past, sir, only once to say that he had known Yorkshire as a child."

"And how did he provide for you?" Lord Failfoot demanded.

"Why, he was a barrister, sir, just as I have become."

"A barrister!" the old man said with a note of disdain in his voice. "And did he leave you nothing when he died, sir? Some memento or other?"

There was a long silence.

"Only this, sir," Mr. Rhodes said at last, releasing the watch which hung across his waistcoat from its chain.

The old man took it in his hands and seemed to cradle it as he made a close examination.

"So it is true then," he muttered to himself. And then, returning the article to its owner: "I gave him that watch, sir, on his coming of age. It was my father's and his father's before him. There was a crest on the back, but I see that he has had it scratched away. It is only one of many signs of his ingratitude to me."

The ice cold of his calm disappeared in an instant, and his face grew scarlet with remembered rage.

"He disappointed me in everything!" he exclaimed. "A thankless, luckless lad!"

"I cannot listen to you speak of my father in such a way, sir," James Rhodes said quietly. "This has come as a great shock to me, and I cannot think clearly yet. But it will not come to this. You shall not libel to my face the best man who ever lived. Good day, sir. I must take my leave before I say more than I mean to."

"Wait. Please, wait," Susan whispered.

But he did not hear her. Indeed, it was clear that James Rhodes heard and saw nothing. Susan saw him reach blindly for the knob of the door, and then, in a moment, he was gone.

# Chapter 16

"La, I think Mr. Rhodes will never forgive either you or Lord Powell," Penelope said, dipping her golden curls into the sunlight which flowed through the parlor of the blue salon. "And, of course, he *should* not. Now that your little intrigue has been exposed prematurely, he has lost his chance with his grandfather entirely."

Susan stared at her sister angrily. When she had suggested that they speak frankly with one another, she had imagined to find that Penelope had some concept of the damage she had done. And yet, here was her mirror image accusing *her* of being at fault for what had happened!

"You amaze me!" Susan said in a low voice. "Never have I seen anyone more self-centered and so completely unable to see life as it really is. These may sound like harsh words, but had I not promised

Aunt Dorothy to keep a close rein on my temper, you would be hearing harsher still."

Although there was no one in the room to comment on it, Susan felt certain that from this day on she and her twin would not be readily confused, for certainly what had passed between them must have left its mark. From now on there would always be something—a turn of the head, perhaps, or a cast of the eye—which would keep them separate. More important than their outward differences, however, were the inward ones. Both of them knew now, Susan was certain, that there could never be any true affection between them.

It made her sad, and yet her determination to say her piece was so great that she could not yield to any form of pathos. She and her sister were unalike. Surely that was not so great a tragedy. The fact that nature had carved them in identical form was an accident and nothing more. It made no demands on their affections. They disliked each other, each of them, no doubt, with cause. Penelope would never forgive her for having schemed to "rob her"—as she put it—of the fortune Lord Failfoot had dangled in front of her. And Susan would never forgive Penelope for having tricked Mr. Rhodes into a humiliating situation. Humiliating, yes, and much—much worse.

For a few moments, after Mr. Rhodes had left, Susan had been so full of regret for what had happened, so torn by sorrow that the young man held her and Lord Powell accountable that she had not noticed what was going on in the room. When, however, she became awake to the situation, she found that Lady Tangle who had, apparently, been outraged to an extent that she could no longer hold her peace, was berating Penelope for her unscrupulousness, while Lady Hammerhead, never one to remain in the background, was defending her charge with all of the shrill-voiced vehemence she was capable of. To add to the general confusion, Lulu and Reginald were at one another's throats, a situation which no one cared enough about to remedy.

The banging of Lord Failfoot's cane brought everyone to attention. Silence fell. It was the first time Susan had looked at him since Mr. Rhodes had taken his departure, and she was shocked at the change in the old man. His face, never full, seemed shrunken and in such a way that one could fancy how the skull of him would look after death. His beady, black eyes seemed to be set even further back into his head, and there was a curious expression, which might have been one of defeat, on his face.

"Get out," he said in a low voice. "Get out, all of you and take your cockle-headed animals with you. I want to be alone."

His voice was a mere shadow of what it usually was, and as the ladies looked at him, he seemed to lose his grip of his cane. At all events it toppled to the floor. In an instant, Susan had hurried to return it to his hand.

"Will you be all right alone, sir?" she asked. "Perhaps I should send Brattle to you."

"Get off! Get off!" he muttered, and as she did as she was told, she saw him close his eyes as though he were too weary to hold them open for a moment more.

And now Penelope had had the gall to hold her responsible for it all. Draped languidly on the crimson and silver striped sofa by the window, Penelope let her fingers play with the curls on Lulu's back and looked at Susan speculatively.

"I think you ought to consider how all of this will appear to Lord Powell when he is told of it," she said in a low voice. "Come. It does no harm to look at what has happened with some objectivity, surely."

"I—I do not think that I can bring myself to do it," Susan said. "We agreed to come here and speak frankly, and I must tell you honestly, Sister, that I want nothing more at this moment than to leave this house and you and—your aunt behind me forever."

"Ah, but we promised both my aunt and yours that if they would keep well away from one another for an hour, at least, you and I would try to come to some understanding," Penelope reminded her.

"I know that," Susan said, restlessly pacing the room. "And I will do so. But I have no interest in looking at the situation from Lord Powell's eyes. I *will* not play those sorts of games. He is his own man and will see it in his own way. But, as for being objective, I am in favor of that above all things. Let us begin with what you have demonstratively done."

"No," Penelope drawled. "Let us be orderly and start at the beginning. Tell me, how did you and Lord Powell determine that Mr. Rhodes was the Failfoot heir?"

"I am not free to disclose that information," Susan replied. "If our granduncle wants to know of Lord Powell's source of information, he can ask him. More than that I cannot say."

"I expect you were delighted at the news," Penelope said with a sneer. "The chance to conspire with such a handsome gentleman as Lord Powell does not present itself every day. And then, of course, you must have liked to know that I would never lay my hands on granduncle's fortune."

"Lord Powell and I brought Mr. Rhodes here because we thought it was right," Susan said flushing. "And so it was. It was a great tragedy that our granduncle quarreled with his son and never saw him alive again. It was an even greater tragedy that James Rhodes was allowed to grow up not knowing that he was heir to one of the highest titles in the realm."

"Not to mention one of the greatest fortunes," Penelope said with a sidelong glance. "How generous of you, Susan. How very generous of you not to think of yourself—or of me—for a single moment."

"You know I did not want to compete for granduncles's fortune in the first place," Susan retorted. "All of which does not mean that I am playing at being good or even that I am sly. I do not like to be manipulated. It is as easy as that, if you would only believe it. But that is by-the-by. Your regard for me or mine for you does not really matter now."

"Very well," Penelope said in agreement. "I will grant that your motives might have been innocent. After all, we are here in this room for compromise. But you were foolish, at the very least. You should have told Mr. Rhodes the truth. He deserved to know it. What an irony that you should be so firm about not allowing yourself to be manipulated and all the time . . ."

"I take your point," Susan said. "You have made it very well. Yes. No doubt I was foolish and unwise, but I had—we both had—James Rhodes's good in mind."

"And I had my own good in mind," Penelope murmured. "But never mind that. The next thing is that you must face the fact that the old gentleman is not someone who can be played tricks with. He mistrusts the world, probably with good reason, and now he mistrusts you, as well. More important, he believes that Mr. Rhodes conspired to be introduced to him."

"He did not do so!" Susan declared.

"I will grant you that you may be right in that," Penelope agreed. "I cannot believe that anyone could put on such a convincing act of innocence as he did. But I am not my granduncle. He, I think, will prefer to believe that he has been used. From the little that he said of his son, you can see that there is great resentment there still. And from Mr. Rhodes's reply, it is clear that he will not let his father be criticized. As a consequence, I think you must accept the fact that, heir or no, the chances of reconciliation between the two are slight."

Susan ran her fingers through her curls, not bothering to hide her agitation.

"But it is not fair that no one will profit from this," she murmured.

"I think you have forgotten me, Sister," Penelope said in a teasing voice. "I took the trouble to protect my interests and I hope you will not think me boastful if I tell you that I think I have protected them very well indeed."

Susan ceased her pacing to look down at her sister.

"You?" she demanded. "I am not the only one who needs to have things put clearly in front of her, I think, if you can believe that now. Now! After all that you have done."

"The old man gave no indication that the contest was to be called off," Penelope said, examining her fingertips. "Things are as they were before. Whoever wins Lord Powell wins all."

"But you cannot think that Lord Powell will as much as speak to you again after he learns of what you have done!" Susan exclaimed. "To have written

181

to Mr. Rhodes and signed my name was bad enough. To have opened a letter addressed to me was, may I remind you, another felony, or would be called that if I choose to charge you in a court of law."

For the first time Penelope threw off her languid pose. "You would not do that, would you?" she demanded. "Where is the letter? Did you return it to the old man? What a fool I was not to get my hands on it during the excitement! I suppose you have it. I suppose you will use it against me."

Susan shook her head. "I remember holding it. And then, I think, I must have dropped it. Wait! I remember. Ah, well, you have no need to concern yourself. I can see Aunt Lucinda now in my mind's eye. She hurried to pick it up. The evidence will be returned to you so that you may destroy it. But it does not matter. I do not need the letter."

Penelope visibly relaxed. Her dark eyes narrowed.

"So you think Lord Powell will believe you when you tell him that you did not send any protestations of affection to his friend," she said in a low voice. "What a high opinion you have of yourself, Sister. Why, I declare, even Mr. Rhodes was not convinced. Surely you saw that. It is easy enough for you to cast me always as the villainess, but others may be more fair."

"You cast yourself as villainess enough when you duped me with Sir Edwin Gingerton," Susan re-

182

plied. "Lord Powell knows of that little trick. He will not be at all surprised to find that you posed as me again."

Penelope pouted for a moment. The languid air was stiff now, assumed. Indeed, as she lay back against the cushions of the chaise longue, she looked like a serpent about to strike.

"I think," she said with a voice full of venom, "that you have made certain errors in your assessment of Lord Powell."

"Have I indeed?" Susan said dryly. "I expect your Continental background makes you much the better judge."

"In this case, yes," Penelope said, trailing her fingers through the air as though she traced a path in water. "You seem to think that because a gentleman finds a lady admirable, he also finds her desirable, and that, I assure you, is not the fact of the matter."

There was an assurance about her voice that gave Susan pause. All this had taught her one thing about her sister, at least, and that was that Penelope's voice changed when she was lying and when she was telling what she believed to be true. There was a certain ring about the latter and Susan heard it now.

"Lord Powell may not *admire* me for having deceived Sir Edwin," Penelope went on, "but he has noticed that I have other charms, I assure you. I have seen it in his eyes and I think the fact that he desires me will weigh the evidence in my favor when he hears it."

Susan felt a sudden chill, although the windows were closed to the breezy day. She remembered that Lord Owens had told her that Lord Powell preferred older women, and of course, the only reason for that must be that they were more experienced. And, although she and Penelope were the same age to the hour, Susan realized that her sister had been taught the wiles of much older ladies and in a French court, as well. How could she have hoped for so much simply because Lord Powell had come to her for advice, had agreed to scheme with her? How could she have allowed her head to be turned simply because he had signed his Christian name to a letter? A single letter! Oh, what a fool she had been.

She calmed herself by dint of clenching her hands so tightly that her fingernails were driven painfully into her palms. She must not allow herself to be carried away by Penelope's arguments. They might or might not be true, after all. Simply because her sister believed that he desired her did not mean that it was true. Neither did it follow that her appeal would make her any more convincing when he heard her story. But he must *not* hear Penelope first, Susan told herself. That spiteful girl had ruined everything for Mr. Rhodes. She must not be allowed to widen the trail of disasters which she left behind her.

"I will make a point of taking Lord Powell aside at Almack's tonight," she heard Penelope say. "It is such a misfortune, dear Susan, that you find it difficult to be audacious. But I will be quite shameless. And I believe that I will be able to convince him of—of anything."

Suddenly Susan's mind was made up. She would do anything to keep Penelope from speaking to Lord Powell before she had had a chance to make him understand the truth.

"Besides, it will be easier for me to approach him, I believe," Penelope was saying with a laugh. "Unless I am mistaken, I think he was annoyed to see you paying so much attention to Mr. Rhodes last night. Indeed, no doubt he thinks you are a flirt."

Such taunting was unendurable, but Susan kept her voice very even and her gaze direct.

"Well, then, the contest is well and truly on," she said. "Shall we drink on it, Sister?"

"Very well," Penelope agreed. "I will ring . . ."

"Oh, do not bother," Susan said. "Once our aunts know where we have closeted ourselves, they might very well descend on us. Besides, I thought, perhaps, for once, a stronger drink than ratafia might be in order."

"In that I heartily concur," Penelope said with some spirit. "Ratafia is such a feeble stuff. I must say, Susan, that I am surprised to see you take what I have said in such good spirits."

"It is only because you have given me some no-

185

tion of what to do and how to go about it," Susan assured her truthfully. "Three minutes. No more than that, I promise you."

In actual matter of fact less than two minutes passed before she returned to the blue salon, cheeks flushed, two half-filled goblets in her hand. They raised their glasses and drank. Two minutes after that Penelope had sunk into such a deep and motionless sleep that Susan did not bother to tiptoe when she left the room.

# Chapter 17

Afterward Susan was often to ask herself what had happened to her judgment that day. Granted that the amount of laudanum she had mixed into Penelope's drink was only that which would be sufficient to keep her sister from being aroused until long after the ball at Almack's was over, but she could never understand how it was that she had been capable of so many wrong decisions in the hours which followed the administering of the drug.

But, at the time, it had seemed to Susan that she only did what was necessary in order to make Lord Powell understand what had truly happened that afternoon. An excess of energy seemed to possess her. Never had Susan acted with more decisiveness. When Lady Hammerhead discovered her charge asleep on the lounge in the blue salon and, finding that she could not arouse her, raised a cry, Susan had frankly admitted to what she had done. She could have lied and said that Penelope had taken the dose herself to quiet a headache and that, doubtless, mixed with the brandy, it had had an excessive effect, but she had no time or patience for such prevarication, at least while she was still at the house on Grosvenor Square. Leaving Lady Hammerhead in a perfect fury, Susan had gone to Lady Tangle's room and announced her intention of attending the ball, adding that her sister and her "other aunt" would not be able to accompany them. Interrupted by Brattle, who came knocking to say that Lord Failfoot wished to see her, Susan had calmly announced that she would see her granduncle tomorrow. Subsequently, she had helped herself from Penelope's wardrobe and, two hours later, presented herself in the downstairs hall, resplendent in one of her sister's most elaborate and daring Paris creations which she only bothered to conceal in part with a long ivory satin cape.

"But what do you intend to do, my dear?" her aunt asked her hesitantly once they were in the carriage. "Why are you acting so strangely? Is it true, as Lucinda told me, that you put Penelope to sleep with laudanum? And why are you dressed in your sister's clothes? Oh, dear! Oh, dear! It is all so much more than I can deal with! Did you really plot with Lord Powell to bring that nice young man into your granduncle's company? Is he in fact the heir? Why is it that I knew nothing of all this? Oh, dear! Oh, dear! I feel like a poppy with half its head blown off. You know how sad it makes me to see them so when summer passes and now . . ."

Susan calmed her aunt as best she could, aware that it would suffice better to answer her questions when she was calmer. As it was, Susan knew from experience, Lady Tangle would forget everything that was told her almost immediately or else make such a dreadful muddle of it all as to make it impossible to unscramble the facts later.

"You must only believe that I know what I am doing, aunt," Susan told her gently, capturing one of the fluttering hands and pressing it. "There is only one thing you must know. Penelope has pretended to be me in the past. Tonight I shall be she. And you must sit in a corner and attract no notice, since if anyone were to realize that you had accompanied me and not Lady Hammerhead, suspicions might be raised."

"Oh, it is not right," Lady Tangle wailed. "I feel it in my bones. It is one thing for Penelope to be artful. She has been trained to do it. But masquerades do not suit you, my dear! Indeed they do not!"

"But did you not cry out Penelope's name when I descended the stairs to the hall tonight?" Susan demanded. "If I can deceive you, aunt, I think I can deceive anyone. And this is no idle gesture, I assure you. I have a purpose which must be accomplished."

And yet she had known even then that she had not dared to have her convictions challenged. This alone would have told her, she reflected later, that she was wrong. But the trip to Almack's took such a mercifully short time that her aunt had no occasion to question her further. Within minutes they were in the grand ballroom and Lady Tangle had made her disappearance into a familiar corner of the sort she often habitated.

Almost the first person Susan noticed was Lord Powell's sister Evelyn, her face wreathed with smiles, swinging by on the arm of the young gentleman Susan had first seen her with. Thankful that Lord Powell would, as a consequence, be at more liberty than he had been the evening before, Susan went in search of him, gliding across the floor in the manner which Penelope affected, and fluttering both fan and eyelashes at any passing gentleman.

Apparently Lord Powell had seen her before she him, for, turning suddenly to let her eyes roam the room, Susan found him standing directly behind her. For a moment she almost let a spontaneous exclamation made in her own voice give her away, but she managed to cover the lapse with one of Penelope's lilting laughs.

"How very glad I am to see you, sir," she declared, moving her shoulder in such a way as to allow the edge of the tiny puffed sleeve to slip down further on her arm. "My sister Susan sends her regards and wishes me to tell you expressly how sorry she is not to have an opportunity to talk with you."

"Your sister is ill then," Lord Powell asked with an air of concern.

190

"No, only quite weary," Susan replied. "She does not have my stamina, you know, and the slightest upset wearies her extremely."

His dark eyes were hooded and Susan wondered whether he thought it wise to mask concern. And, at the same time, she found herself wishing that she had never determined to deceive him. For he *was* deceived, of that she was quite certain. She should feel triumph that her plan had succeeded so well, and yet she was aware only of a certain emptiness, as though she were a hollow shell.

"And may I ask what has upset her?" he asked with a frown.

Again Susan laughed in Penelope's tinkling fashion.

"Indeed you may, sir," she said. "I think you have a right to know. How naughty it was of you and Susan to keep me in the dark concerning the real identity of Mr. Rhodes."

Lord Powell was clearly startled by this announcement, and taking Susan's arm, he drew her to a corner of the room.

"What do you know of Mr. Rhodes's identity?" he demanded then, almost roughly.

"Why, if I say so myself, sir, I believe I have been very clever," Susan replied, fluttering her eyes as she knew Penelope would have done. "I ought not to tell you of my part in the affair, I'm sure, since you are certain to blame me. Yes, I think I have been too outspoken already."

"And you will be even more so before you leave me," Lord Powell muttered.

Suddenly Susan knew that what she was doing was wrong. Wrong and unforgivable. It had only seemed like a practical idea when she had conceived it in the heat of temper and with the knowledge that her sister was well and truly dangerous. She had told herself that she must act boldly, but this—this charade had nothing of boldness in it. Indeed, it was an act of cowardice.

"I think—I think that I must leave you now," she said to the gentleman glowering down at her. She knew that he had reason to be angry, since she had just told him that she, as Penelope, shared the secret of his friend's identity. But even though he thought she was her sister, she wished she had never had occasion to look at her in just that manner.

"And I fear I must restrain you, Miss Collins," he replied grimly, "until you tell me precisely what has happened."

She wanted to confess that she was Susan then. No matter how angry he might be when he found out that she had deceived him, it would be better than this. But he gave her no opportunity.

"How come you to know anything of Mr. Rhodes's affairs?" he demanded.

"I—I spoke to him at length last evening, before the first interval," Susan replied, realizing that his urgency demanded that she must continue as she had begun. But she would get it over quickly, she promised herself, and then make her confession.

Lord Powell's questions came like gunfire.

"What did he tell you?" he demanded.

"That he had never known anything of his father's past and that his father's name was James and—and other things. Enough to permit me to guess the relationship between him and my grand-uncle."

Lord Powell's dark eyes seemed to search hers.

"And how did he happen to be so intimate with you," he demanded. "when, to my certain knowledge, you and he had never spoken more than a few words together? It is your sister Susan he knows better."

"He—he thought that I was she."

"You mean you told him that you were Susan?"

"Yes."

"And do you two often exchange personas when it suits you?"

There was a scornful note in his voice which made Susan feel sick at heart.

"No," she said. "It is a despicable thing to do! I know that now!"

"It is a fine thing to be so honorable after the fact," Lord Powell said dryly. "Now, once you had this insight, what did you do about it? Come, you began this conversation by suggesting that you had been very clever. Do not play at modesty now, I pray you."

Susan took a deep breath.

"I—I thought it wise to tell my granduncle," she murmured, "since it was clear to me that he was being manipulated."

"Another honorable gesture," Lord Powell said. "Will there be no end to them? Tell me, how did you go about it?"

Susan realized with a shock that she could not tell him about the forged letter, for if she did, he would want to know why she had found it necessary to put both Susan and his friend in the wrong. Then she would have to tell him about her granduncle's scheme and how it involved him. He must never know that. Never! If he did, he would be so filled with disgust. . . . Even if she were to point out to him, later, acting her own self, that she would scarcely have promoted Mr. Rhodes with her granduncle if she had wished to play the game, he would never forgive her for not having warned him, for having encouraged him to come to the house in Grosvenor Square.

"Why do you hesitate?" Lord Powell demanded. "Come, you must tell me everything. I insist on it."

She could not defy him. Everything in her rebelled at doing so. And so it all came out about the letter. And he listened in an expressionless manner which filled her with dismay.

"Indeed you have been clever, Miss Collins," he said when she had finished. "You must be very proud of yourself indeed."

Even though she knew he thought he addressed

her sister, Susan felt a deep anguish. But he was still speaking.

"And why was it so important to you to put my friend in the wrong?" Lord Powell said in a low voice. "His inheritance, if it should have come to that, robs you of nothing."

"I—I cannot tell you!" Susan cried. "Oh, I have been wrong! So very wrong. I must only say what should have been said at first and that is . . ."

"So you flinch at the last minute," he said angrily. "Your cleverness has been too much for you, Miss Collins. Miss Susan Collins!"

So he had known of her charade from the first! He had known, and yet he had let her go on and on, weaving herself more and more tightly in her own web. Susan stared up at him in dismay. And then, with a little cry, she turned and fled.

# Chapter 18

"Oh, my dear, my dear, whatever is the matter?" Lady Tangle exclaimed as Susan hurried her into the carriage. "We just arrive and then you leave and you dressed in Penelope's gown! I declare, it has put me in such a state!"

"It will be all right, Aunt Dorothy," Susan said in a voice which belied her agitation. "I have made a grave mistake. One I can never put to rights. But I must put all that behind me. I will deal with the others honestly, and then let us put London behind us."

"You mean we will return to Somerset?" her aunt cried. "You know that I would like nothing better. But it will mean cutting the season short for you, and your Mama . . ."

"If Mama were here now," Susan said, her voice

197

breaking, "she would understand why we must go. London was never the place for either one of us."

"Perhaps you are right," Lady Tangle said faintly. "But I do not know what has happened. What mistake has been made? What do you mean by speaking honestly to the others? But no! Do not try to explain. My head is in such a muddle that I would never make sense out of it."

Susan was glad enough of the chance to remain silent. She could not bear to think of what had just passed between her and Lord Powell. Perhaps later when it did not hurt so much. . . . But for the present she must steel herself for what must follow. She could not slip away from the house in Grosvenor Square in silence, although it would, by far, be the easier way. She had practiced deceit once and with such unfortunate results that she knew she must never dabble in it again. Cleverness had cost her happiness. Cleverness had cost Mr. Rhodes his inheritance. She could do nothing now about the first, but she knew she must do all that she could to right the second. She owed herself nothing, but she owed Mr. Rhodes everything he deserved.

She had dreaded the thought of attempting to assemble the household in the drawing room, but as it happened they were there already. Even Penelope was seated, heavy-eyed, beside her aunt on the sofa, while Lord Failfoot with bottle in hand sat facing them, his gouty foot propped high.

And they were quarreling. Standing just inside the door of the long room with her aunt behind her,

198

Susan found that they were so caught up in their dispute that they did not notice her.

"I cannot think how you should find it amusing that Susan should have duped my niece as she did, sir!" Lady Hammerhead was saying shrilly, her turban casting its usual ominous shadow on the wall. "To have drugged her and then taken her clothes! I cannot think of it without wanting to take the gel in hand. Why, I shall give her such a boxing about the ears as to make her wish she had never thought of such a thing."

"All's fair in the sort of game I have proposed," the old man declared, cuffing Lulu with his cane and taking a deep quaff from his glass at the same time. "She'll make a fair way with that fellow Powell tonight, damme if she wont!"

At that Penelope began to wail and Lulu to yelp. Susan moved forward and Lord Failfoot looked up in amazement.

"Why, here's the clever chit herself!" he exclaimed. "So much accomplished in an hour! I would not have thought it possible! Has Powell offered, then?"

"No, he has not," Susan said in a level voice. "Nor will he ever. I have come back to explain just what I have done and why. It is not a pretty story."

"I should not think it could be!" Lady Hammerhead declared, rising to her feet. "Why, you deserve . . ."

"I have already received all the punishment I deserve and more, I assure you," Susan replied. "I need no boxing of the ears to make the point. Let me begin by apologizing to you, sister. It was a cruel thing to do, and I will not attempt to defend myself. Your gown will be returned to your wardrobe as soon as I have finished saying what I have come here to say."

"You pretended to be me," Penelope said in a dull voice. "How could you have done such a thing?"

Susan did not remind her that she had done the same, not once but twice. Who was she now to make accusations? But Penelope must have bethought herself of what the ordinary response would have been, for she flushed and fell silent.

"Well, chit, get on with it," Lord Failfoot declared. "You've a deal of explaining to do to me, damme if you haven't."

Susan noted that the bottle on the table beside him was half empty. It was difficult enough to determine what his mood was, let alone how much the claret was responsible for it.

"I do indeed owe you an explanation," she said in a low voice. "But I will begin, I think, by explaining why I went off as I did tonight. I wanted Lord Powell to know the truth, and I was foolish enough to think that he understand it best if he were to think he heard it from my sister's lips."

"That's an odd notion, given the gel," Lord Failfoot declared. "But go on! Go on! What was all this truth he needed to know?"

"I doubt that he heard much of it," Lady Hammerhead said grimly. "To think that . . ."

"Let the gel speak, dash it!" Lord Failfoot roared, applying his cane to the floor with his usual vigor. "I've heard all I want to hear from you this past hour, madam. Take my word on it."

And so, while Lady Hammerhead fumed and paced and Penelope languished, Susan proceeded.

"I told him that his friend's true identity had been revealed and the circumstances surrounding it," she said.

'You told him about my letter?" Penelope demanded in a blurred voice. "You pretended to be me and you told him what I had done?"

"Just as I thought," Lady Hammerhead declared. "In the name of truth-telling, your sister has tried to blight your chances with him!"

"That was not my motive," Susan replied.

"And I suppose you told him about your grand-uncle's scheme to award his fortune to whichever of you might win his regard?" Lady Hammerhead went on. "Oh, how like you it is, Susan, to spoil everything."

"I did not tell him that," Susan said defiantly. "And I am ashamed of myself for not doing so. But it seemed such a terrible, unscrupulous story that I could not."

"You take such admirable pains not to soil your fingers," Lady Hammerhead said scornfully.

"It was not that," Susan told her. "I cannot explain. Besides, just at that moment when I might

201

have done so, he told me that he had known all along that I was—that I was who I am."

"Caught out, were you!" Lord Failfoot roared. "Set you back on your heels, did it?"

"That is one way of putting it, sir," Susan replied. "I knew long before that that what I was doing was wrong."

"La, you were forced into it!" Lady Tangle exclaimed, advancing to the center of the floor with a quite unusual boldness. "You were never one to twist and turn the facts until you were set an example. And we all know by whom!"

"No, Aunt," Susan said gently. "I made my own decision. I made my own mistake. I have no one to blame but myself."

"Raggle-taggle!" Lord Failfoot declared. "Lot of women's fuss over nothing. Gel plays a silly game and gets her comeuppance. Happens every day, I warrant."

"It was still wrong," Penelope said dully. "And for me as well as Susan. Can you believe me, Sister, when I say that I am sorry. I mean that all the games I played were done out of spite."

"And greed," Lady Tangle announced, a suddenly formidable figure despite her bonnet which was all aslant and her flushed, round face. "You could think of nothing but the fortune."

"Fortunes were meant to be thought about," Lady Hammerhead said as severely as a headmistress teaching an important lesson. "A gel's a fool not to think of her future."

"I think I have thought too much of the future and too little of the present," Penelope said slowly.

"You are suffering the effects of the laudanum." her aunt said sharply. "Your wits are muddled. You will think more clearly tomorrow. For the moment it would be best if you said nothing."

"Perhaps," Penelope said sadly. "Perhaps. And yet it seems . . ."

"Back to the point!" Lord Failfoot interrupted her. "Now, we've heard your sad story, chit, tell me another. What did you and Powell mean by bringing my—that young gentleman here under false colors?"

An incredible weariness settled over Susan, but she knew that she must see this through to the finish.

"Lord Powell knew of Mr. Rhodes's true identity from the start," she said. "His grandfather told him before his death because he thought that someone should know."

For a moment Lord Failfoot seemed to shrivel in his chair. The cane fell to the floor, and he made no attempt to regain it.

"So that was it," he muttered. "Arthur told him, did he? Eh, even as a lad he could keep no secrets. Damme if I had known that he had seen my son in London. Recognized him. He should have written to me. I deserved to know."

Susan felt a sense of sadness. How could she tell him that Lord Powell's grandfather had kept silent because Lord Failfoot's son had sworn him to it?

203

How could she let him know that, even to the last, James Rhodes had been determined to keep his true identity secret?

"I am certain that he thought he was doing what was right, sir," she said in a low voice. "Perhaps he believed that you would never forgive him for whatever it was which separated you from your son."

"Forgive," the old man muttered. "Forgive! Who's to know what I would have done."

"At all events," Susan went on slowly, "Lord Powell confided in me as soon as he knew that you were my granduncle. And he expressed a belief that it was a great injustice that matters had turned out as they had. He asked me if I thought that a reconciliation might be possible. And I said I thought it might, if only you were to meet your grandson with—with no prejudice on either side. If both of you could come to know the other simply as people. And then, when you had come to like and admire one another . . ."

"The matter of the disinheritance was settled long ago!" Lady Hammerhead cried. "You had no right to interfere!"

"Oh, do be quiet, Aunt," Penelope demanded. "I grant I thought as you did when I first heard. Aunt Dorothy was right when she said that I could think of nothing but my own gain."

"Perhaps Lord Powell and I were wrong not to be more direct," Susan said to the old man. "But James Rhodes never knew what we were doing. He

204

came here unawares. There was no pretense in his liking for you."

"We played chess," Lord Failfoot muttered. "Taught his father myself, don't you know. Young Jamie. Yes, young Jamie. All so long ago."

Susan looked at him with concern. He seemed to ramble. Never had he showed his age so clearly. Could it be that even in this she had made a mistake, that it was all too much for him?

"A barrister, he said," Lord Failfoot said with a start. "And Jamie before him. 'Pon my word, his mother would have been proud to know he made something of himself. All on his own, don't you know?"

Something about the pathos with which he spoke struck silence even into Lady Hammerhead. Susan waited. They all waited.

"He left me angry," Lord Failfoot mused.

"You mean your son, sir?" Susan said softly.

"My grandson," the old man declared, suddenly attempting to pull himself from his chair. Brattle, who had been standing in the shadows, rushed forward to help him.

"Only because he thought you meant to criticize his father," Susan declared. "You must remember that it came as a great shock to him to learn so suddenly who he was. And it was a shock to you, as well. Both of you spoke hastily. That need not be the end of it."

"It was the end of it once," Lord Failfoot

mumbled. "Said he never would come back. Closed the door. T'was the last time I ever saw him."

He was standing now, a quaint figure in his pantaloons and ancient frock coat with his periwig tilted on his head. He leaned heavily on Brattle's arm.

"But young James—your grandson—never said he would never come back," Susan reminded him. "And doors were made to be both closed and opened."

"Yes, yes, you are right," Lord Failfoot muttered. "I am an old fool. But not too old to learn a lesson. Write to him, gel. Ask him to come to me tomorrow. And I will be prepared. Either way, I will be prepared."

Susan went to kiss him gently on his forehead, and Penelope, too, rising heavily from the sofa, did the same.

"It will all come right," Susan told him. "Believe me, sir, it will all come right at last."

# Chapter 19

Susan had not been at Tangle Hall for two days before she realized that it was not possible to retreat from the world that simply. She might ride her horse for hours across green velvet meadows, leaping streams and stiles and racing the wind at a gallop until she was breathless, but she could not escape her memories. She might ramble the width and breadth of the estate with her dogs until the moon rose high in the sky, but she could not forget the look in Lord Powell's eyes when he had told her that he knew she was not Penelope.

It did little good for her to remind herself that she had been honest with the others. Before she had left London, she had written to James Rhodes as her granduncle had asked her to, urging him to see the old man again and adding her regrets that she should have had any part in attempting to manipulate a situation. But no word had come to her and her aunt in the country either from anyone of the household on Grosvenor Square or from Mr. Rhodes himself to let her know what the outcome had been. As for any message from Lord Powell, Susan did not attempt to deceive herself that such would ever come.

As for Lady Tangle, happy as she was to be at home with her familiar things about her and no more need to sit in drafty corners of London ballrooms, it was clear that she was concerned about her niece.

"Try not to be so restless, my dear," she told her. "You did what you could to help poor Mr. Rhodes and I am certain he is grateful for it."

Susan could not tell her aunt what was really troubling her, for if that lady were to even guess that Susan's heart had been broken, she would have been beside herself with concern.

Hour after hour, alone in her room, Susan asked herself what would have happened if she had acted differently from the start. When Lord Powell had first told her about his friend's relationship to Lord Failfoot, she could have urged him to tell James Rhodes the truth at once. It had, after all, been her idea to introduce the young man to her granduncle simple as an acquaintance of Lord Powell. If she had given other advice and Lord Powell had seen fit to follow it, grandfather and grandson might never have met. Or, if they had it would have been as strangers, one of whom would have seemed simply to be seeking his rightful fortune. Lord Failfoot would never have known whether or not he was being pandered to. There would never have been that game of chess, she thought, for Lord Failfoot would have assumed that it was simply another way of his grandson's attempting to ingratiate himself. At least, as things had turned out, both young man and old knew that they had liked and respected one another before either knew what was at stake.

How useless it was to reflect on what might have been, Susan told herself impatiently. Running down the servants' stairs in order not to disturb her aunt who usually took the opportunity of the quiet hours after lunch to snooze a bit in the sitting room, the girl hurried out into the courtyard which sheltered the kitchen garden and called for the dogs. Two were hunters and they came bounding toward her from the stables while Reginald made his progress in a more dignified manner, as befitted his breed.

Promising herself not to give way to idle speculation, Susan took the path which led to a grassy hill which lay to the west. The sun was bright. Swallows swooped overhead. The air was fragrant with the scent of flowers. Before she had gone to London, this would have been all that was needed to make her happy. And now . . .

There were so many things she could not have prevented. Certainly her announcement that she meant to take no part in her granduncle's scheme to set her and Penelope in competition for his fortune and Lord Powell had done nothing to make him change his mind. And she could not have anticipated that Penelope would be so clever as to draw the connection between their granduncle and Mr. Rhodes. She could not have kept herself from falling in love with Oliver. Yes, she *would* call him that in her thoughts! Even though she would never be able to say the name aloud.

Susan awoke to the realization that she was doing precisely what she had promised herself not to do. Oh, it was all so hopeless! How absurd it had been of her to think that simply by returning here she could become the simple girl she once had been. Dropping down onto the grass, Susan wrapped her arms about her knees and stared blindly at the passing clouds.

The sun was dipping into the west when she made her return to the ivy-covered manor house which rested so snugly in the valley. The hunters bounded ahead, but Reginald, as though sensing his mistresses's distress, kept very close to her.

Knowing that she must change her grass-stained muslin gown and wash her tear-streaked face before she presented herself to her aunt, Susan hurried into the house through the kitchen door, only to encounter May, the under housemaid waiting for her in a state of some excitement.

"Wherever have you been, Miss Susan?" the girl exclaimed. "Why, you've been wanted in the sitting room for the past hour! Your aunt is quite beside herself! You must go in to her at once!"

"I must tidy myself first, May," Susan declared.

"Tell my aunt that I will be down in a few minutes."

And, hurrying to her bedchamber, Susan set herself to rights, wondering all the while why her aunt should be in a state, since, by now, she must be accustomed enough to Susan's leaving the house for long stretches at a time. Having changed her muslin gown for another and scrubbed her cheeks until there was some color in them, Susan descended to the sitting room only to discover that her aunt was not alone.

"Well, my gel!" Lord Failfoot announced. "You've given me a pretty wait, and your aunt here has been flying up into the boughs. What do you say to that, eh?"

Susan was so surprised to see him that she could make no reply. Although less than a week had passed since she had last set eyes on the old gentleman, he seemed quite changed. Although he was slouched in a chair in his usual manner, there was no longer any bandage about his foot and there was an air of vigor about him which had nothing to do with the ill-natured state she had associated with him in the past. As though symbolic that some change had occurred in him, his cane was propped peacefully against a nearby table. Reginald, who had followed her upstairs, puffed across the floor to greet his old friend by lapping one wrinkled hand.

"Good dog, that," Lord Failfoot declared. "Well, miss, I expect it would be too much to hope for you to greet me with a kiss. Altogether too much, eh?"

A look of satisfaction spread across his face as Susan came to salute him. "Mind my wig, gel!" he warned her. "There now, that's better. Everything as it should be and bound to be better."

Taking Susan's hand, he drew her down to sit on the footstool at his feet. For the first time since she had entered the room, Susan had an opportunity to look at her aunt who did, indeed, seem greatly agitated. Murmuring something about ordering tea, she hurried out of the room, casting about herself with her fan.

"Tea," Lord Failfoot grumbled. "Well, I expect I can put up with it for once. Now, what about you, gel? That aunt of yours tells me you've been out of sorts since you came down here. Worried about you, she is. Can't have that, you know."

Susan found her tongue at last.

"I'm quite all right, sir," she said. "And glad to see you, although it is quite unexpected. Have you decided to leave London and return to Yorkshire?"

"That's the way of it," the old man told her, beaming. "Have to show my grandson around the old place, don't you know. Sooner he takes the reins in his own hands the better."

Susan took the old man's bony fingers and pressed them between her own.

"Everything is settled between you then!" she exclaimed. "I cannot tell you how glad that makes me."

"Thought you'd be pleased," Lord Failfoot said

212

happily. "All due to you and that fellow Powell, you know."

At the mention of Oliver's name, Susan felt the blood drain from her face. There was so much that she wanted to ask. Had her granduncle seen him? What had he thought when she had left London? Had he known why she had run away? And did he care?

But she knew that the old man would have none of the answers she wanted most to hear. And she knew as well, remembering the way he had looked at her at the last, that it was only folly to want news of him. And so, to cover her confusion, she asked of Penelope and Lady Hammerhead instead.

"Thriving, both of them!" the old man declared. "Nothing like an eligible Viscount to make those ladies happy, don't you know? Send you their love for what that's worth. You'll know that better than I. But, damme, we have better things to talk about. The fact is, Jamie's waiting to talk to you in the garden."

For a moment Susan did not know who he was making reference to, and then she realized that he had given his grandson the same affectionate nickname that he had given his son.

"But what is he doing there?" Susan demanded And then, inconsequentially: "Does Aunt Dorothy know that he accompanied you?"

"Damme, of course she knows," Lord Failfoot replied. "Explained the whole business to her while we were waiting for you to turn up. Not that I

213

could get a word of sense out of her in return except that I think she hopes it may perk you up a bit."

"What may perk me up?" Susan asked him in confusion.

"Why Jamie's offer, gel! Jamie's offer! There's nothing a gel likes better than a proposal, or so I've been told."

"A proposal!" Susan murmured in dismay. "But surely, sir, you do not mean . . ."

'I mean what I said," Lord Failfoot assured her. "My grandson is waiting to declare himself for you. Don't stare at me like a lobcock. Off you go to join him! Tea, pah! We will have champagne to celebrate!"

# Chapter 20

Susan found James Rhodes waiting in the rose garden. Not having heard her approach and, no doubt, worried by waiting, he sat, bent forward, on one of the benches and drew pictures in the gravel walk with a long stick. Perhaps it was her imagination, but Susan thought there was a certain air of dejection about the slope of his shoulders and the hang of his head.

Nevertheless, as soon as she spoke to him, he leaped to his feet and smile most pleasantly as he made his bow.

"How delightful to see you again, Miss Collins," he said.

"I had not dared to hope to see you again so soon, Mr. Rhodes," Susan said, simply uttering the greeting which form demanded and hoping that he would not take it otherwise. "Oh, dear. I should not call you Mr. Rhodes any longer, I suppose," she went on, helplessly.

"I am accustomed to the name," he told her. "And since, in fact, my father legally changed his own, it is in fact mine until, of course . . ."

He broke off and Susan knew it was from delicacy that he was not more explicit, since he would not become earl until his grandfather died.

An awkward silence settled down between them. Susan was torn as to what to do or say next. Should she inform him that Lord Failfoot had announced the reason for their visit and that it had thrown her into utter confusion?

"I am so pleased that you and your grandfather have made it up between you," she said finally. "It is the only right thing."

"I did wonder, at first, if I had done the proper thing," Mr. Rhodes confessed. "I mean my father did die adamant. I have asked myself time and time again whether he would have wanted this to have ended as it has."

"Your father's quarrel is not yours," Susan said gently. "He could not make it up, but given the circumstances, no doubt, he would have understood why you should make peace with your grandfather."

"That is precisely what Lord Powell said to me," Mr. Rhodes said gratefully. "I am so glad you feel the same."

Another silence, this one longer than the first. Susan thought it would never end.

"This—this is not simply a casual visit, Miss Collins," Mr. Rhodes said finally.

"I—I understand you and my granduncle are on your way back to Yorkshire," Susan said quickly, instinctively attempting to delay the moment when he would offer for her.

"That is not what I mean," the young man said, turning scarlet. "I have come for a particular reason and that is to . . ."

He fumbled with the words, and for the moment, all seemed lost.

"Before you go on," Susan said quickly, "will you tell me whether it was your own idea to make this visit or your grandfather's?"

"Why, perhaps he did suggest it," Mr. Rhodes muttered. "But I assure you . . ."

"And did you feel that you must honor the suggestion because of the letter you wrote to me in response to the message my sister sent you in my name?"

James Rhodes stared at her helplessly. "There was that to consider," he replied. "After all, I did make certain implications . . ."

"But only because you did not want to humiliate me in what appeared to be a bold declaration of affection on my part," Susan reminded him. "Your letter may, as a consequence, be forgotten. I have forgotten it. You must feel no need to do what might seem to be the honorable thing."

And all the time she spoke she remembered that he had said that Lord Powell had given him the same advice that she had. That meant the two had talked together, probably at length. Which meant, in turn, that Lord Powell probably knew that he was coming here and the reason for it. And yet, apparently, he had not recommended against it. It was no more than she should have expected, and yet the realization was painful to her in the extreme.

"My grandfather told you what to expect from me, I see," Mr. Rhodes said suddenly. "It took you by surprise?"

"The idea had never crossed my mind," Susan assured him.

"And now that it has?"

"Lord Failfoot is a great eccentric," Susan said in a low voice. "No doubt you will find him equally full of strange notions in the future. I think you must resist them, sir. And it is well to begin as you mean to finish."

An expression of relief lightened the young man's features.

"You mean you do not think I ought . . ."

"Indeed, I am certain that you should not," Susan told him. "If it were your own desire to do so, of course, you should not be prevented, even though the answer would be the same in either case."

Susan was afraid that she had been too enigmatic for a moment, since Mr. Rhodes seemed to ponder the remark with considerable earnestness.

"It is strange, you know," he finally said in an

artless manner, "that you and Lord Powell agree on so many things. When he heard that I was coming here and the reason for it, he said much the same thing."

Susan felt herself begin to tremble. To avoid giving evidence of this, she sank down on the bench.

"Still, I felt I must do it," Mr. Rhodes went on as though talking to himself. "There was the letter to consider, you see. I had no way of knowing how seriously you took my response, although you only took a moment to glance at it when my grandfather handed it to you. And then he would assure me that you had only come away to the country because you wanted me to follow. He considers himself something of an expert in the matters of the heart, you see."

"I expect he does," Susan said with a sigh. "I fear that your future with him will be very difficult, sir, unless you offer the occasional challenge."

"And, as you said before, I should begin at once," the young man said with energy. "Yes, I see that is the only answer. I will go to him at once and explain. . . . But how shall I put it?"

"If I were you," Susan murmured, "I would begin by saying that, in such important matters, you must follow your heart. And since, on this occasion, your heart did not command you . . ."

"Yes, yes. That is excellent," Mr. Rhodes replied. "I think I can make him understand."

"I will help you if you like," Susan said, starting to rise.

"No, no," the young man said quickly. "You must stay just as you are. That was the arrangement, you see."

"The arrangement?" she asked him, bewildered.

"The arrangement I made with Lord Powell," Mr. Rhodes said, almost impatiently. "It was his idea, you see, that he follow grandfather and me here. If my proposal were to meet with an acceptance, he would quietly return to London. A signal was arranged. I will make it now. He is waiting with his horse at the end of the drive. Thank you, Miss Collins! Thank you for having been so understanding."

And with that he was off, pausing on the steps of the manor house to wave one arm recklessly before he disappeared inside, no doubt intent on remembering precisely how he would begin his explanation to his grandfather.

Susan did not rise from the bench. She felt, somehow, incapable of movement, although, at the same time, her senses were more than ordinarily alert. The scent of the roses was overwhelming, and the warm breath of the breeze on her cheek was like a caress. The sound of the buzzing bees nestled in the hearts of the flowers seemed to drown out all other sounds. And yet she knew that if she could break out of this prison of immediate sensation, she would hear a horse's hoofs on the gravel drive.

She closed her eyes and when she opened them he was standing very close, looking down at her with those hooded dark eyes she had seen so often in her dreams.

"So," he said, without preamble, "you have refused him."

"It did not come to that," Susan replied barely able to control the trembling of her lips. "I did not think it right for him to make an offer which he did not mean."

Impossible to read his expression. He took a step forward. His head became a silhouette against the sun.

"But if he had meant it? If you had not been able to prevent him from speaking? If he had been ardent with you?"

"I do not love him," she said simply. "He is a fine gentleman, kind and sensitive. But were he to have every virtue in the world, I could not love him."

Reaching down, he took her shoulders and raised her to her feet. And then released her. They stood very close together but without touching.

"Tell me this," he said in a low voice. "If you had loved him, could you have forgiven him anything? A tendency to sudden anger, perhaps? Lack of understanding?"

"Yes," she murmured. "Yes, I could have forgiven anything."

"And, had he loved you, could he have forgiven guile, impetuousness, deceit?"

"Yes," she said again.

There was an urgency in his eyes, and Susan knew that it was reflected in her own.

"Then can we forgive one another?" he asked her. "I was angry too soon. I did not try to understand."

"And I deliberately attempted to deceive you."

"Does all that really matter?" he said in a low voice.

"Nothing matters but this moment," Susan told him as he drew her close into his arms.

His lips touched hers lightly at first and then with increased warmth. And then a sudden shout made them draw apart. To Susan's amazement she saw Lord Failfoot hobbling toward them, supporting himself heavily on his cane. Behind him came his Mr. Rhodes, and Susan was relieved to see that he was grinning. At the rear Lady Tangle followed, waving her fan distractedly with one hand and attempting to right her mobcap with the other.

"So this is the way of it?" Lord Failfoot demanded, coming to a halt and striking a rosebush with his cane. "Saved me a bit of trouble if you'd have told me from the start, gel."

"I think I say for certain that we knew only this moment, sir," Lord Powell said with a slow smile. "If we have put you out in any way, I am sure we are sorry for it."

"Put out! Put out!" Lord Failfoot declared. "What sort of muckworm do you think I am? Nonsense. If Jamie is not to have her, then you will do

222

nearly as well, sir. Damme, I only came to offer congratulations. Now, come along! Come along! Serious matters to discuss and all that. And champagne all around!"